THE LONELY YOUNG & THE LONELY OLD

stories by Tim Miller

The Lonely Young & the Lonely Old by Tim Miller

ISBN: 978-1-938349-79-9
eISBN: 978-1-938349-84-3
Library of Congress Control Number: 2015948048

Layout and book design by Tim Miller and Mark Givens

Cover photograph:
"La Villette, fille publique faisant le quart, 19e. Avril 1921" by Eugène Atget

lyrics reprinted for "Climbing High Mountains" [traditional]. The author's thanks for the version by Blind Willie McTell

Thanks to the following magazines where these stories first appeared:
    "One Time People": *Juked*
    "Adult Conversation": *Meat For Tea*
    "The Lake": *Foliate Oak*
    "Flew Away for Number Three": *Bitter Oleander*

First Pelekinesis Printing 2018
For information:
Pelekinesis, 112 Harvard Ave #65, Claremont, CA 91711 USA

www.pelekinesis.com

The Lonely Young & the Lonely Old

stories by Tim Miller

Also by Tim Miller

Hymns & Lamentations

To the House of the Sun

Bone Antler Stone: Poems from Old Europe

for Jenny and Evie

Contents

For the lonely young and the lonely old,
for the hungry rich and the hungry poor,
for the sick in body, mind, and spirit,
for the weakness in all of us, we pray to the Lord.

—Catholic Marriage Rite

Holy Dread

I'M NOT A VIOLENT PERSON, I HAVEN'T BEEN FOR YEARS, IT TOOK YEARS TO FIX that in me and not even a minute to ruin it, but he put his hands on me, you don't put your hands on somebody. And he acts like he doesn't know me, real serious, like he believes it, in front of the customers too, so I look like the idiot, like I'm crazy or something.

I turned around and looked for some of the familiar customers but none of them were there—and why would they be, I was coming in early, I only know the people who come at night. But he wouldn't let me behind the counter, says to stay back, to stay back or he's calling the police, and I said, I called him by his name and I said *Stop messing around, you know I start in a half hour*, and kept on walking behind the counter and past the registers, and that's when it happened, I felt his hand on my shoulder and he's grabbing my shirt and pulling me back, not even saying anything, just pulling and tugging on me, and I wasn't expecting it so I fell back and up and turned around and faced him, and the people in line were snickering, they were laughing because I'd fallen over—so I push him, I pushed him, I did, I said *What's your problem, do you want me to go home?*, and I asked where the manager was.

I've only been working there a few months but that's no reason for this, to have him try to throw me out, humiliate me in front of people. I knew he never liked me, but this is a bad joke, and bad for him too since he wasn't going to have my help for the next eight hours. But then I saw some guy come out of the cash office with a register—some guy I never saw before carrying a register, and I say, *Who the hell is he?* And the guy doesn't budge, doesn't notice me, just smiles and walks by.

And the asshole who made me fall on the ground is breathing all heavy and he says he's calling the police and I yell to him *But I work here! I work here! I'm on the schedule! You know me!* And I don't know how he pulled it off, he's the fakest guy I know, he was a shit the first second I met him, some guy who can only talk about football and his truck and what he's doing with his yard, and if you can't talk about those things he's got nothing to say, and since I hate sports and barely have a car and only got an apartment I had nothing to talk to him about, so he never said anything to me. And I'm different now, I make a point to talk to people if I can, to at least try, I used to be like him but it got to where nobody liked me, so I had to open up, but he never did. And here he is, me yelling that *You know me, You know me,* and I knew he was a horrible liar too, but he was still able to yell back—this a guy who never lost his cool, he lost his cool for real here—he yells, *I've never seen you before in my life, if you don't get out I'm going to call the police, I'm going to call the police!*

And his dumb ass wants to lunge at me, he wants to follow me outside, I see it in him, he wants to fight, but not because he's playing a joke on me or because he really hates me—*he's all hopped up and angry because he doesn't know me, he's pissed off at some crazy stranger*. I see it in him, I know because I've felt that way towards people, I know the look and how it feels. In that moment I understand him, but in the same moment I crumple into myself and I hunch over and I leave, I just leave. And I stood outside the store for awhile, not knowing what to do—I mean, I have bills to pay, rent, phone, I've got to eat, I need money, I need my job. But they say they don't know me.

* * *

I take my car and I drive to the other side of the plaza and I wait an hour or so and then try to call the store. I try to use my cellphone but my password doesn't work to unlock it, which is ridiculous, I use the same four numbers in my password that I've always used, but whatever—and I walk to a payphone and call the store. I ask for the manager, and when he's not there I ask for the guy in signs—real good at making signs, and he comes in after everyone else and wouldn't have been there for the scene before—and I've talked to this guy a million times, he's got great stories, he used to be a dancer for somebody like fifteen years ago, he went on some huge stadium tour with him, I know he likes me, and I say hi to him, I say *Hey, what's up*, and he comes back with *Who is this?* And I say my name, I say *C'mon, you know me, we've talked for hours on slow nights, you know me*—but he gets all defensive, makes it sound like I'm spying on him, says he doesn't know where I heard about him, but to leave him alone, because I'm talking faster now and saying everything he's told me, and he just says to leave him alone, he doesn't know me. And I nearly start screaming at him, but I'm in front of a grocery store, there're people and their kids walking by, cop cars in the parking lot, the mail truck pulling up—all that, just some afternoon—and a guy screaming into a payphone gets attention. I mean, I want attention, but not that kind of attention. So in mid-sentence, him still talking to me—he sounds scared, really scared, at what I know about him—I just hang up, I hang up.

I walked back to car then. I'd feel it a million times after then, but that walk to the car—past the families and the housewives and the guys gathering carts and the friendly yells of people to other people they knew, the sounds of cars and the sounds of trucks and doors shutting and the sound of music from the cars, or the sound of just the bass, or just of people laughing, talking, laughing, dreadful— I began to feel like I was floating, like no one could see me. And as I went, I tapped on the cars as I passed them, and I saw a little kid walking with his mom stomping on the ground and smiling, and I did the same—I made sure I was still here. It sounds ridiculous, but I sensed even then that somehow I wasn't. Like I said, I'm not a violent person, it's been years since I ever did anything like that, and after that first lashing out at the guy at work, there wasn't any more of it, I couldn't go back to being that way, I crumpled into myself instead, whatever, I'm not saying either one is better.

When I got back to the car I tried getting the cellphone to work, but the same thing. I went to the cellphone place in the plaza—I mean, that's why I got one of their phones, it was so near where I worked, where I bought groceries, and all of that was near my apartment, I knew if I had a problem I could just walk over there on lunch or before a shift. I tell them I can't unlock the phone, can't use it, and he acts all helpful at first and says he'll look right into it, just needs my name and address, to see my license, and I show him and he types all the info in but says he can't find me, says he can't find me—and I start to crumple again, and back away from the counter, but he doesn't understand yet and thinks it's a computer glitch and goes back to his manager with my phone. They're back there for awhile, I can watch them, they take the back off the phone and are looking at something, the serial number, and in time they look suspicious, and when the guy walks up to me with his manager, I know they know, and the guy says (and I know the game, his manager standing behind him "in case something happens"—but they don't know that I'm not like that anymore) there's no record of my account, and not even of my phone, and that if this is a pirated phone, something illegal, and he's stuttering (some kind of test for this kid to act stern in front of his manager, the world is so sad), and he wants to know where I got it, and I just grab it from him and run from the store, run to the car, I drive home, I drive home even though I know what I'll find there.

And it's true—I stop at my mailbox first, I smile at the lady getting her mail, too, but get no look of recognition back, and when my key doesn't work and I begin to look suspicious, she grabs her mail quick and goes away. I walk through the complex to where my place is, and I try the key there—it slides in, but doesn't unlock. I jiggle the handle, but nothing, I try again, and just as I do the door's pulled open, and some guy is just standing in my apartment, smiling at me. I can see behind him that it's still my apartment, everything is where it was, *everything is where I put it, it's all mine*, but instead I'm facing this guy, and he's the one inside. But he doesn't look suspicious or even alarmed, he just smiles at me, doesn't say a thing, and it hits me—the guy from the store! The one who came out of the cash room with the register! But that's impossible, he's back there at the store. But here he is in front of me, still not saying anything, not saying anything. I finally mutter something stupid, *Is so-and-so here*, the first name I could think up, and he says he's sorry, but I have the wrong apartment, and he closes the door. Nothing about why I was trying to get in, why I thought I had a key to his place, he just shuts the door.

I stand by the door awhile longer and hear him moving around in my place, finally I hear him start the shower. I run fast as I can to my car and drive back to the store. There's no way he could've made it out of the shower and to his car and back to the store before me, the road was mostly empty anyway as I drove—again, I knew that, that's why I decided to live there, it was close to work and close to the city but still outside a bit, nearly in the woods, some trees, the trees and the birds that I love, all things that're now just dread, terrible dread, because when I get to the store I don't have to wait more than a minute before I see him in the front window, helping a customer at the copier. There's more than one of him, somehow, and yet there's none of me. I'm not here, I'm not here, it's ridiculous.

* * *

I go through the rest of my options—I try to fill up my gas tank, I go to the pump and try to use every credit card I have. None of them work. I throw them away. I have cash on me, but not much. By now it's getting into sunset, it's getting dark. I know what I'll have to do later, but I have to wait until the store closes.

I knew I'd get more cash later, so I go to the thrift place in the plaza and buy some more clothes—I can't walk around in my work shirt all day, and I can't get my actual clothes from my place, so I got a few things. Then I went to blow some time at the bar, and it's there I almost break down. I'm new here—moving again, moving all the time, I just got here, new job, new shitty car, new apartment, I don't know anybody, the first night I was driving by and I found this bar. The place is a college town, so weekdays it's filled with kids who use up all their energy studying, then the rest getting drunk and hooking up, it was a revelation to me, I thought when I first found the place I'd hate all the kids, I'd hate all of them, but I didn't, I didn't. They were endearing and innocent, even the guys who'd fucked a hundred girls by now and barely in their early twenties, even the girls who thought they were women and already had a regret list a mile long—even these saps were still innocent, they weren't hardened yet, they knew no great tragedy, no great suffering, and they would only become not innocent when they realized their youth was nothing but tragedy and suffering, nothing but tragedy and suffering not because of what went on, but because they were ignorant of the depth of what was going on, they had the experience but missed the meaning. I should know, I only got to sixteen before that all crashed in on me.

And I don't drink, the only drink that gets me drunk is seven dollars at a bar, and the version of it you get at a bar is watered down, so even I would need a handful to really get drunk, and I made friends there, with all of them, they had me try beer and I'd nurse some huge pint for three hours, and they'd all push up against me when it got crowded, laugh at me at the bar as they were getting their thirds and fourths and fifths and I was still on my one, my one getting cold, but it was all good-natured—I was older than them, they got something out of it, knowing someone older than them that wasn't their parents or a teacher or a boss or some authority, they could see I wasn't the usual person.

But not anymore, I'm not anymore, I'm not anything anymore. I saw all of my familiar faces, all of them, it was a curse that night, that dread, to see not just a few of them but all of them, everybody was out, and none of them said hello to me, none of them said a word, none of them said a word. And I was in no position to introduce myself, it took so much to do it the first time around when I first got here, so I just sat there trembling with a beer I couldn't drink, looking around at every pair of eyes, hoping just one of them would recognize me, remember me, say hello, know who I was. It had taken me so long to get better, to be able to talk to people, to open up, to be able to listen and to go out and to meet strangers and not be petrified, *and I was doing so good, I was doing so good!* And now this. Nobody. Nothing.

I tried an experiment, and I closed my eyes and counted to a hundred, closed my eyes and counted another hundred, up to a thousand, I counted slow and slower, tried to keep one hundred as far away as possible, hoping someone would ask me who I was, what was wrong, why I was sitting there with my eyes closed. I felt them all pressing up against me, ordering more drinks, I heard the band (or not a band, just some old blues guy in the corner with an amplifier and an old guitar and black sunglasses on and a foot-drum), I heard a jukebox, I heard all of their gossip and all of their flirting, but none of this was for me. I put my money down and left.

* * *

I went back to the store. The night shift people were in, and I knew by now they wouldn't recognize me. I had a notebook in the car and a pen, and brought those in and sat by one of the tables anybody could walk in and use, I used to laugh at these people, treating our crappy store like an office and using the free phone and the free tables and they'd end up leaning back and scratching their heads or even rubbing their bared bellies or propping their feet up like they're at home, and now look at me, I'm one of them, one of those people I thought was pathetic. Now I'm pathetic, if I'm anything. And I thought I'd use the notebooks as props, an excuse to sit there for awhile, but I actually did start writing something. Or diagramming, drawing, scribbling. I tried at first to figure out what had changed between me leaving my apartment in the morning and me showing up at work to start my shift, I went over it and over it in my head until I realized I didn't remember being at the apartment last night, or even the night before, or at all this week.

How this didn't occur to me earlier I don't know, but it was as if I was pushed through a huge open door and into a great darkness, I hardly remembered anything, and whatever this was had been going on for a long time. I didn't remember anything for the past week, I didn't understand time anymore, who knows, the memories I did have could've been from months ago, so much was just a blur. I wrote it down, I wrote it down that I remembered being in the apartment and spinning around like I'd done in the kitchen when I was a kid, and that I'd stopped at one point (this in the first house, before we moved) and saw the hallway juggling and spinning itself in front of me, and in the hallway I saw the definite shape of a grey figure, bobbing back and forth because I was still dizzy. I remembered being somewhere else (a restaurant counter?) and seeing the unmoving shape of some person, its back to me as it stood in front of something, a revolving map rack. I remembered being outside in a nearly empty parking lot and seeing a person far away, underneath lamps that didn't work, yet still visible from some source of light I couldn't see, the outlines of something grey and unmoving—

And I jumped up when I remembered this, and turned to the parking lot outside. Nothing, of course. And not that the memory meant anything, it only made me more sick and more scared, more sick and more scared, it cleared up nothing, nothing. I still looked up at my coworkers and saw no sign of recognition on their faces. I scribbled more notes, and I thought, and I kept my eye on the clock.

When the place was about to close, I waited for them both to start cleaning—one of them bent down behind the counter, and the other one went to the other other side of the store by the computers, and I got up and took my things and slid over to where we take passport photos. It was the first thing that confirmed that I really was here, that I really was here, that what I remembered was real, since I knew that the store had been a million others things before it was a copy shop, and they'd kind of improvised the passport area and put it the only place they could, and that somebody could hide behind the screen unnoticed. I knew this because they'd told stories about scaring each other around Halloween doing just that.

And I found the spot, I could've cried out at knowing I was real, I was real, all just because this dusty spot behind a screen was also real, but I just hid and stayed silent, I waited for them to finish their cleaning, to count down their drawers, to turn off all the machines, to gather their things, to set the alarms, to leave, to lock the doors. I waited, I waited ten more minutes, and then burst from the spot and began running. The motion alarm started immediately, and I made it to the back door where one of the keypads was, and punched in the right numbers, the same numbers I punched in every night to close the place down, *the same numbers I punched in every night to close the place down*, and the alarm stopped. It hadn't been on for more than five seconds. I went into the cash room and opened the safe with the same combination I used everyday—*the same combination I used everyday, I'd been here*—and took all the cash from all five tills, all the change, all the money, more than a thousand dollars, went to the back door, re-engaged the alarm, left the store and found my car and drove as fast as I could. They wouldn't open again for another nine hours, and I wanted to be far away by then. Thankfully, I thought, even if they got a description of me from the camera, or if there were cameras outside in the parking lot to get any description of my car, or even if they found fingerprints, they wouldn't be able to find someone who apparently wasn't here.

* * *

There was only one place for me to go, only one place to go to see how far this had gone. It was a straight twenty-four hour drive, but I needed sleep and slept in the car in the parking lots of hotels, I showered in the showers at the big truck stop plazas, I looked around at people. And as I went, and just as I began to chat with the waitress, just as I started to forget what was happening, or to watch the news from a TV dangling in the corner above a counter and pretend to be one of the rest of them, I would turn and see that grey shape—by a t-shirt rack, leaning over a stack of newspapers, its back to me sitting in a booth far down the restaurant, or standing far away on a bridge. And in the faces of strangers I saw the face of that kid, that guy, the one in my apartment and the one in my job, the one in *my* job, the one who smiled but didn't say much, who seemed unperturbed and unconcerned. I saw them both everywhere, and they were dreadful to me.

And as I drove further I slowed down, I took it easier, I knew if I was caught for stealing the money it might be a blessing, and if I wasn't, all the better, and I didn't want to get pulled over for speeding. It had nothing to do with running. Whatever this was, like the grey figure, it was about stillness—or like the face of the kid, unmoved and not worrying. And as the sun rose one morning—how many days later I couldn't say, I'd gotten off the highway and had stopped for hours in places before continuing on, I had no idea when it was, what day or month—I woke in the car in the parking lot of some all-night restaurant that overlooked the highway, and I watched a car down on the freeway run another car off the road and into the wall of an overpass. It happened that simply—I opened my eyes and sat up and saw it, the flames and paramedics and the police, and I thought of my brother, my poor brother, the one I'd killed years before—or not killed, but been respon- sible for his death, but happy at his dying, and I think in the moment maybe I actually did intend to kill him. He was younger than me, and quiet, and I was older and always in trouble, I didn't understand life, or death, I was so sure everyone was against me, and when we drove one night in winter on the highway and I got mad at him he just stayed calm, and I wanted his calm and I wanted the love and the sympathy he got from our parents, it was as if he wasn't my brother at all, or their son, he was so different from all of us and we all knew it, like some aberration thrown into our lives, and they loved him for it, none of dad's rages, none of mom's breakdowns, it wasn't always that way but it came to feel like it, and he had none of my violence, no drama, he just carried on. And we had a shitty car then just like I do now, and I thought to kill us both, to take him with me, it'd look like an accident on the freeway, bad car and bad tires on the ice and snowing bad, and somehow I found the right place and headed for a wall, the same kind of wall under a bridge, and cut the wheel at the last moment so we spun and crashed—though he was killed, not me with him, and everyone mourned what they said was an accident, or just stupid teenage driving, and all of my rage and need for rage seemed to go with him, and no one blamed me, not even with their looks, I mourned and cried for what I'd done and not actually for him, which made it worse, but they took it as mourning for him and never blamed me, let alone accused me, and I've been tired and tiring and unable to do much since, other than crumple.

And as I drove I tried to remember my brother's face, I tried to remember my brother's face, I tried to remember his silhouette as he stood or sat, just my brother's face. Did either of them match the face of that kid in my apartment and my job and who knows where else, did either match that grey figure? Could it be that easy, a simple matter of retribution and guilt? I tried to remember his face and his shape, I tried to remember his face and his shape, but I couldn't, I couldn't. I couldn't deny it, the guilt was all there, but only for doing a bad thing, not a bad thing to a certain person, and that meant more guilt for not feeling the right guilt, for not confessing, for being a coward and never confessing—and I'd thought about what I'd done a thousand times, but never thought about who I'd done it to. I'd forgotten everything about my brother the moment my car hit the wall, and I'd been happy to, I was still happy too! What a horrible person I'd been, what a horrible person I still was, I thought that was all over but I was still the same—what horrible premonitions I had when I was a child! Nothing ever changed, all dread.

And as I drove and drove, how I wished to remember his shape and his face, to make sense of what was happening now. But it wouldn't come. He eluded me as I had secretly always wanted him to. I was still jealous of him, still hated him, and had spent all the time since his death justifying what I'd done with how I lived, which is impossible to do. Only now, as I drove, did I understand the confusion and the dread at that I would find when I pulled into my parents' driveway, since only that dread seemed to justify what I'd done. Or at least give me something equal to what he'd felt, going out in early youth for no reason other than being more decent that most, and having an idiot for a brother.

* * *

And when I found their house, finally, I realized I'd been driving slow to avoid getting here, not for some nobility or fatalism of *Come what may*, I was just a coward who'd wasted his life and deserved what he would find at his home and his door. I got out of the car, leaned around and locked all the doors from the inside, threw the keys inside, and shut the door. There was no place further to go from here, no matter what I found. And I knew what I would find.

What I found was the house in fall, a huge tree in front of my old bedroom window burning a bright orange and carpeting all the front yard with its changing leaves. What I found was the rusting basketball hoop and rusting chain net, unused for more than a decade—and as I walked by, I refused to look at the concrete I'd help lay to set the pole in the ground, afraid of the initials I knew I wouldn't find there. What I found was the two upstairs windows facing the street—my room, and the room of my brother—visibly insulated with plastic and heavy curtains, signs of an aging couple whose kids are gone since this is what they do to the windows of rooms they no longer use. What I found was the lawn and backyard whose grass I cut for years. What I found was the mailbox by the street in the shape of an old farmhouse, a link to the city's rural past and still rural surroundings, all the covered bridges everywhere, and I cursed myself that I should have found a few of them before coming here, they were so peaceful. What I found were the gutters just beginning to overflow with rain and leaves, as always. What I found were a dozen spots in the driveway, and a few more near the front door, in the lawn, all around, where family photos had been taken in the past, me in my baseball uniform or me with a homecoming date, me filled with horror and disgust and rage but making a go of it, trying to try, trying to try, just trying. What I found was a yard of railroad ties and old mulch and the same garden my mother puts up every year, the hose and the water, the rusting house numbers by the front door and, turning, the sound of the wind through the trees, that tree of orange leaves but also the ones already bare, and the bushes, the grass unblowing and still crusted with frost, that great terrible dread. What I found was home, but it was not mine.

My mother met me at the front door—I had been pacing outside looking at everything, and she opened the door to see what was happening, and I turned sideways to her and put my head down so that her face might be a blur above the top of my glasses, so that I didn't have to see the look I knew was there. Yet I still reached out to her, turned sideways and my shoulders low and my legs getting weak and great tears in my eyes and an awful muttering from my mouth, like first sounds from the womb, *ma-mothe-ma-moth*, no whole words coming as I reached out but stepped away, and I finally looked up to see her, face older now since I'd gone, face not the fifteen years gone but a million years, a million years because I didn't see her age slowly as I should have, I didn't stay, I only knew her in her late forties and now suddenly in her sixties, an explosion of age that horrified me, my mother never looked this way—but it was her, it was her, her with the grey hair she'd accepted and no longer tried to color, her body smaller from being older, her eyes recognizable in a body recognizable with face and hands and wedding ring recognizable, but from her eyes was none of that recognition for me, none of that recognition for me, none, nothing.

I muttered some more and my legs gave out and I fell at her feet and would have held her waist if I'd had the courage, I said I'd done horribly, I said I'd paid, I said how do you not know me, I said you held me, I said I sat with you in the chair, I said I lay my head in your lap for hours as you combed my hair with your hands and now nothing, I said these things through tears and she understood none of it, I may have only said it all in my head, I may have screamed and cried it at her. And she became alarmed and called to my father and he came to the door to see what was the matter and when I saw him I straightened and sobered up and I put out my hand to my father but he told me to get away, to get away, to go away, what's happening here: *Who are you?* my own father yelled, and suddenly I saw past them, and between them I saw inside the house, inside the house as I remembered it being, since of course they haven't gotten any new furniture, and the furniture they have came from my grandma's house after she died, they were never big on expensive or fancy things or new furniture, it was all so familiar, it was all still as I knew it, all still as I knew it, if I could only return there as I'd once lived there—and I saw pictures on the walls, the same pictures I remembered, and I knew who was in those pictures, and I tried to rush in to see them, I tried to rush in to see them, and

I screamed and somehow could not break loose from the grip of these two old people, and finally my father let go of me and ran to a bookcase, and I ran towards him to see the pictures—but I stopped when I remembered what he kept on the bookcase, and as he raised the gun to me and I ran to him I turned briefly to see an early photo of us all, before everything became horrible, when we were all still happy, my mother seated on the right and my father on the left, both in their late twenties, and between them my brother, young and still fat between them, young and still chubby like a baby, this picture something fancy for us and from a department store, and I could see and feel my mother fixing us all up in our clothes for the day, I could see my father grumbling about having to do it at all, I could see my brother and I laughing at the family comedy, of the grumbling complaining dad and snippy insistent mom, all of us new to being a family, all of us before anything horrible went wrong for everyone, and with my father's gun in my face and my mother screaming nearby, I was not in that picture any longer, I was not in any of them, and so who was my father firing at?

I Become Breathless

I said to God, I said, *God, you took my mother from me, but you've given me back my son.*

That's what I said, what I prayed.

I said, *God, you gave my mother a good long life, now please give me a life with my son.* Because it's only because she died that he's coming home.

I could hear it in his voice, he was upset.

He regretted leaving.

He regretted he wasn't here with me when this happened.

I could tell, he felt guilty, hearing about it over the phone, hearing me cry.

He regretted leaving, and didn't know how to say it.

He's always been so quiet, but I've always known what he means to say. He knows his father was not an emotional man, he knows he's an emotional boy, he knows he would've been there to hug me, he doesn't like what he's done.

(He takes after me, we both cry like babies.)

I'm so excited, he'll be coming before the wake, he'll be with me for everything, he'll be coming in tonight.

I just need to go to mom's house and clean up a bit. Sometime all of us will go through it and separate everything out and sell the place, we'll all have some of her photos, it'll be so nice, we'll all have some of her in our homes, on our walls. But today it'll just be me.

I can be myself with her, I'm almost there now.

* * *

I saw these little girls in the store today, they were just adorable, so little.

One little girl was bringing over a bathing suit to show her friend, her sister you know, and one would find a new one and the other would close her eyes so she could be surprised, they were so happy.

I would love to have had a girl, but I'm happy with my son.

I used to think, when he would really hurt me, he'd talk back or we'd yell and fight about what he was doing and how I didn't like it, how it wasn't right, I would pray, *A girl would never treat me like this, I should've had a girl*, but then I remembered, a girl would be even worse!

I've seen how girls his age are, they're worse to their mothers. It must be terrible for mothers with daughters. Dealing with boys isn't great, the ones who think they're men. He thinks he's a man, he got drunk once with his friends before he left, that doesn't mean a man.

He's something else.

He's still so nervous, he's so unsure of himself.

He's always been so quiet.

When I told him I was going to the store today, he said he goes there all the time, they have twenty-four hour ones down there too. He said he goes there at night to watch people. He says he listens to them. He said he must've gone last night because he was thinking of me and mom, and he made me cry.

No son remembers those things except the ones who love their mothers.

Because after his father passed, my husband, after he passed, and then after my boy moved away, what I did on Saturdays was go to the store and call mom. We would talk for hours, I would tell her what I was getting, we would be talking even after I got home.

She couldn't get out much then, and I didn't want to be at home alone on a Saturday afternoon, so I went out and I'd call her, we got along so well.

I miss her so much.

But I'll see him and he'll be with me. That will mean so much.

I remember when he went out to get his first job, he didn't know how to act, the test he took asked him if he ever stole anything.

He didn't want to lie, he said he had, though he only meant a pen from somewhere, a small thing, he didn't know what they meant.

He didn't tell them that, though, and at first didn't get the job. I told him how stupid he was, I said *Go back down there now, go back down there right now*, and he did, he got the job after he explained himself. They let him take the test again.

He's so unfit, he's unlike me or his father, his father didn't know what to do with him.

There's no reason he left, all he can make are eggs and spaghetti on the oven.

He says he goes grocery shopping, I can't imagine that! He can't keep a budget, can't make out a list, all he does is read.

A book is one thing, but it won't keep you fed, I can't see him organizing anything, I worry so much about him.

I didn't teach him how to use the washer and dryer, does he even wash his clothes? He must. And what kind of washers do they have down there, the kind everybody uses, anybody can use it, those apartment buildings are so filthy.

He probably pays somebody to do it, what a waste, he doesn't have that kind of money.

* * *

I can't wait to see him.

But I'm pathetic too. He's right, he went to the store looking for me and mom. I went looking for mom, and for him.

I saw a little boy just like him, his dark hair, his mother pulled him up from a car-seat and into her arms. How he clung to her. I want him to cling to me, I want to be clung to.

I saw another little boy laughing like him, he ran around a corner from the magazines and had a candy bar. Whenever I took him shopping with me he would go to the magazines to read, even at ten, always the car magazines or the baseball card magazines.

Now he reads God knows what.

Him and his reading.

And I went looking for her, for my mother. I see her in any woman talking on a cellphone, because that should be me talking to her.

I never would've gotten a cellphone otherwise, only to talk to her, I need to ask him how to cancel mine, I don't need it. I'll just talk to him on the regular phone, and he said he'd show me how to use the email, I'll try that, anything to stay in contact with him.

But I'll need a computer for that.

Or I see an old woman outside on a bench, waiting for one of the boys to bring her cart out, and that's my mother, the old woman who clearly has children who love her and care for her, who lived long with her husband.

I won't have that. My dearest was dead before he was fifty. My only son moved a thousand miles away.

I can't wait to see him, I feel so lonesome, I left the store without buying anything and ran to the car where I could cry in peace.

Oh God, because I don't have any of them.

My brothers and sisters all have their families, nobody else is a widow, none of my brothers have lost their wives. And their children are all normal, they've gone to college or are on their way, they live right nearby.

They don't miss mom nearly as much as I do.

When I think about her I am out of breath, I drive through her neighborhood and she isn't there, not there walking on the sidewalk to church.

When we would all get together, she would sit in the center and glow, all of her children around her, and all of their children around her, and she couldn't get around so she would just sit there and stare off and smile at everybody, she glowed.

And how will I ever have that, I *want* it so much. I won't remarry, I can't talk to a man like that ever again, I can't do those things, I'm too old now anyway for any more of that.

And he's had girlfriends, sure, but he's no father, he'd be a terrible father, I love him to death but he needs my help for everything, he should never have children.

I might have my brothers and sisters to sit around with,

but they'll have all of their own grandkids running up to them, they'll all glow, but I won't.

I miss him so much, he should've gotten the earlier flight, I should've offered to pay for it, but now he acts proud about things when I offer him money, as if he isn't just my boy.

Maybe he got the late flight so he didn't have to be with me. What time is his return flight?

I don't have any way of checking, that's all on the computer, but his return flight seems early too.

I'm was afraid to ask him, he'd say something about work, he just got that job (it took him long enough, I was so worried), or he'll clam up.

He's so quiet.

I want to talk to him.

I want to get through to him, I want to tell him how he should be, how easy it would be for him and for me to be happy.

But I don't want to be too much.

I know I'm right, but I don't want to be too much, he's so sensitive.

I'll push him away, he's so sensitive, *But God*, I pray, I keep praying, *help me to get through to him*.

* * *

But I'm here. The house is something else, I'm glad no one else came with me, I still took off my shoes even though she's not here to check.

But she is, of course.

She left the checkered tablecloth on the table in the kitchen, and I pull it off and run my hands over it, the cheap wood.

I don't know how she and dad did it, their birthdays and ours were always near a holiday (mine right around Christmas), so we always celebrated, we never knew we were poor.

I was so clueless about things until I went out to work, I thought everybody was like me.

She still kept the nativity scene up all year, on top of the TV. And all her grandchildren's toys are around that, it's one of those old TVs that's just huge, she never wanted a new one.

On the couch is one of her crossword puzzle books, a pencil is still in there holding her place, but I don't want to look at that.

Right above the Bible she always kept nearby, there's everybody's photos. I look for me and my husband, my son, the three of us.

There must be fifty photos here, three frames, how many gatherings, Christmas and all, but the three of us aren't in any of them, not together anyway.

Some of me with my sisters, or my husband and him on the couch, but not of the three of us together.

They never liked coming here, they were alike like that, I didn't like that, I could never understand.

They didn't want to be around anybody, he probably left to just be alone, but I always wanted a bigger family, that's all I ever wanted.

Although you could say it's my fault we never had anymore.

I secretly blamed him for so long, I would never say it out loud.

How many years I was quietly angry at him, but I didn't know how to tell him, accuse him, how to bring it up, that there might be something wrong with him. It wasn't until after he died that I found out it was my problem, I couldn't have had anymore even if I found somebody to have them with.

What made me the most angry though was that he never minded. We never talked about things like that (who can, and how would you anyways?), he never seemed to care that we only had one child.

Maybe that would've been different if we'd had a girl, maybe he would've been more active or caring or curious if we'd had a girl, since he wanted a son so bad, and what a disappointment ours must've been to him.

All he ever wanted to do was have sex, that was enough for him. That's fine with me, especially when I was younger, but after a while there was no point. Why make love just to make love, something has to come out of it, I mean it can't just be fun and that's it, I hate anything that thrills you for a moment, but I can't find anything else right now.

I hate these photos. In one I see my sister with her newborn son, in another he's grown and she's at his college graduation, her and her son and her husband, her other children, his friends from school, I don't have any of that.

He was in college for a year, if that. He doesn't have any friends, or any friends I want to know about, they probably all do drugs.

When I die, when I'm dead, who will go through my house like this?

What hope will I have? How wonderful that all of my mother's things will be spread out into everybody's house, but all of my things will only go to him, and he won't even want them, I wouldn't want him to have them, he wouldn't know what to do with them, he doesn't know what I like, or why I think things are important, he pastes photos on his wall with no frames, how trashy, he wouldn't know what to do. He has no decorating sense except for putting books on a shelf.

He'll probably throw everything I have away, and what did I buy all of it for, to end up in the trash? I realize now I hate washing things, I've become sick of washing things, clothes and dishes, they just get dirty again and I have to wash them again.

* * *

I pass through the next room, that's where the Christmas tree goes, it's the biggest room in the place that's so small already.

But her bedroom's over there, I can't go in there.

I'll go upstairs instead, it's so sad, to be the only one here, it's so quiet.

There's no railing, the steps are so narrow already. It is so hard to believe I was young here once, all of us were, so many children.

I sat coloring on these steps on Saturdays, since the sunlight would come in through the window in the afternoon, and everyone would run by me, they would all call my name from everywhere in the house and try to get me to go outside to play with them, sometimes they'd even tease me, but there was nothing I liked better than the empty quiet stairwell and the sunlight, and my coloring.

And yes, the Virgin, she was always there. At the turn in the steps in the tiny table, the same one, with the same statue of the Blessed Virgin on it. I would finish coloring and lift it up and show it to her, everyone made fun of me, Mary doesn't want to see your coloring, but mom encouraged me. She said David danced in front of the Lord, I can color and show my pictures to Mary.

I miss her so much. She didn't mind that I was quiet or liked to be by myself. She was the only one. If I'd never married and lived with her I would have never made myself change.

There are a few bedrooms up here, and an extra kitchen, we all squeezed in here somehow.

I go to the first bedroom to sit down. Everything is so small, so old, we got by on so little.

He's so ungrateful, my boy. We grew up on so little here, my mother and father had so many children, and in this small house. We were happy.

Before he became too proud he asked why I didn't support him, I mean I didn't give him anything when he left, it's not like he graduated or got married and was going to buy a house, he was just up and leaving, I won't celebrate that, I won't support that, none of my money's going for that, you've got to be kidding.

I said I won't give him a dime to leave me, and I said how poor I was when I was growing up, and he said he was going off and would be the same way, he said other parents would help out, but I wouldn't even help him pack, I won't support that.

* * *

See, *this* is what I'll support, what I'll remember. All of mom's old dresses, still here. How old are these? How old is this closet?

The wallpaper is peeling off, the same wallpaper since

the house was built.

These dark, peeling corners. All of us growing up in this house, this means something, the flower pattern on the wallpaper I would see every time someone opened this closet.

I pull the clothes aside to stare at the wall, the wallpaper, and there's a ragged bit of it just beside the door. I'll take that home with me, it will be something good to have—but a few things fall to the ground when I tear it away.

They look like little folded receipts, put there on purpose between the ripped wallpaper and the wall. I unfold them and I cry out and look around—it's his handwriting, my son's: what I think are four book titles, and beside each one four dates, doing back twelve years, thirteen.

I feel like I've found a key, I can tell him I found these, sure I don't understand it, but he's always been particular about dates, finding things, writing them down.

I suppose I have been too (if we have anything in common)—I used to write down when we did things or went somewhere, almost like a diary, and then I'd mention it a year later, two, something to think about.

Maybe he did it for the same reason, I could show him this. Maybe we could talk.

After my husband died and the two of us came here for the holidays, I noticed he would disappear for an hour at a time, he said later he liked to come up here because it was quiet, he liked to look at the old things.

And he put these slips in the walls, but he didn't tell me that.

Are there more of them?

I get up to look, but I stop.

I'm afraid. When I used to ask him what he was doing up here, and he would say *Looking at old things*, I could tell he wanted to say more. I knew he wanted to say more, but he never did.

Did he think I wouldn't understand?

But I want to understand. Maybe these are like pictures to him, when I see pictures I remember the whole day. Maybe when he sees these, and remembers his books, he remembers the whole day, we aren't so different, really, they're just books.

Maybe I'll just show him these, and if he says there are more, we can come back here and find them together, that would be so wonderful, to do that together, to be here together.

That's what I'll do, we'll have dinner at the airport and I'll bring these from my purse and we'll talk, I'll talk to my son.

But I stop again, between the stairs.

He used to keep a diary, and when he was ten my husband and I went to find it and read it once, when we thought something was wrong. And he was so angry when he found out, I forget how he found out.

Would he be angry I found these?

He doesn't get angry, but when he does it's terrible, he's even more quiet, he sounds like his father when he's fed up and yells, I hated the sound of it when he got angry, too.

I can't have him be quiet. I need him. I miss him so much.

I can't risk pushing him away, I love him, I need to know he's still mine, he came from me, he doesn't understand that, he doesn't understand how I still remember that, I become breathless when I remember that moment, when he came from me and I heard his cry, when I knew I had someone from God, a gift, my mother was there with me and she later said the sound I made when I first held him was as if he had been missing and there was a chance he'd never be found, not the sound of meeting someone who had been with me the entire time, but things are so hard for me and that's just how it felt, it felt even in that moment that I could lose him if I wasn't careful, and I felt so a part of things and so blessed when he was first put in my arms, my husband there to see it, all of us together.

Now I just tear at myself, I turn to Mary and I pray, I cry. What should I do? What should I do? I don't need to be this sad, even if he is so far away, we can still talk. Things don't have to be like this.

* * *

I don't know how long I've knelt here.

I check my watch and need to get to the airport.

I can't do it. I can't think about it anymore because I don't have anymore time. And I can't do it, I can't take that chance.

I go back to the closet and put the slips back where I found them. I'll forget about them. I'll let them go. I have enough to remember already, that will have to be enough.

Flew Away For Number Three

MOMMY WANTED A NEW DADDY AFTER THEY PUT DADDY IN THE BOX AND then the box in the grass.

Mommy wasn't home because she was looking for a new Daddy, she said another one would marry her, we heard her at night.

We never saw the new Daddy, Mommy never put him in the car here, he would be on her phone and she yelled when we saw.

We talked about him and Mommy put marks on our bums and our faces, and put stings there with her hands. She swore bad words.

She smelled like bad water and smoke when she came home. She tried to say things and sounded like us. She didn't sleep in her bed and was on the couch.

She forgot to give us supper, and said school said we didn't have to go there.

We thought it was vacation, we laughed when everyone else was on the bus, and Mommy locked everything and we couldn't go outside at all, we wanted to go outside. The windows were too tall up for us.

We had no supper too long, so we tricked Mommy. The places in the kitchen were too tall up. We stayed up all night and by the door. We saw what she did all the time. She came in and opened the door and went pee and came back and closed it. We knew she was home from the door opened and the wind inside. This time we went by the door under a blanket. She forgot to see us and it was dark. We waited until she opened in and went to pee, and we went outside. She went to pee and we were in the woods soon. She didn't yell for us for a long time.

There was no food in the woods and we were cold. We got tired. We slept by a tree until it started to move. There was a lady in the tree and she came out of its tummy. She said she lived in the tree and she was all white. She came out of the hard part in the middle of the tree and said we could come in there. We went in there and it was warm in there and bigger than the tree looked like.

We watched the outside but nobody saw us in there.

The lady who was all white said she was always here. She had seen us other times.

She said we could stay or go.

We said stay.

We watched people come through for us. People in jackets called our names. They had dogs.

We didn't answer, since then we'd go back with Mommy, and no supper. The lady who was all white gave us honey and made us laugh. Her hands had fire and we were warm.

We stayed with that lady until the snow wasn't there and the grass was.

The lady said we could live in a tree too. The lady said we could pick one out and go there.

We said we wanted to be in the same tree.

The lady said no.

We said no, we said we wanted to still be with each other.

She said did we want to go back to Mommy. We said no, she made us sting and hit us and left us no supper.

She said we could be animals and could all be together, but that it might be bad.

We said we liked animals.

She said if we wanted to be deers, she would change us.

We said make us deers, and when we were, we ran around.

We had all the supper, we ran and were warm all the time, and we were together all the time. It was like how we were with Daddy, but Daddy wasn't there.

We even stayed out when it snowed again.

We were outside forever, and always had water. We pooped outside and no one said anything about that. We chased and were big and we were warm. It was all fun. We saw cars sometimes but didn't want to be there.

We saw Daddies with guns and always ran away. But one Daddy came and shot me and I was dead. But I was still there and went where my deers body was took. When I went it was like flying.

That was two bodies for me, I thought I would fly until I got a third.

Where he took me was to Mommy's. This was her new Daddy, and he was showing her to me.

She saw me but didn't do anything. She closed the door.

The new Daddy cut me up and yelled.

Mommy came out then.

New Daddy took my dress out of my deer belly. The lady who was all white put it there. It was all red but it was my dress anyway.

Mommy cried and yelled.

Mommy yelled louder.

The lady who was all white left my eyes in my deers head.

Mommy saw my eyes.

She yelled more and fell down on the grass.

Mommy kept seeing my eyes, but I flew away for number three.

Don't Think I Don't Know

DON'T THINK I DON'T KNOW. FROM BEHIND I LOOK LIKE A BOY. I'VE ALWAYS walked with a little hunch, with too much movement in my shoulders. It's worse when I'm in heels, even tiny ones, because I hate heels and my balance is seriously way off, so my shoulders work in there even more, I swivel to keep from falling. The women who walk in six-inch heels that I see in the morning trying to cross the street looking stupid and stumbling, I'll laugh at them, I hope for more potholes, but I'm no better, I'm just as dumb, just in smaller heels.

And I could grow my hair out longer but I don't know what to do with it, I never have. I don't carry a purse or even a cute bag, just a messenger bag. At lunch I fling the thing over my shoulder and onto the table and I feel like someone in a movie, some scrappy girl living on the streets who only has this bag (yeah, like living on the streets is a "scrappy" situation at all, like it's romantic), or a girl in some thriller who's got the answer to some secret in there. I hate how loud it is, how it sounds when I untangle myself from it and toss it on the table. But it's the only thing that carries all my stuff. And it zippers shut, everything else stays open, or it's a backpack, or it's those useless bags girls carry in the crook of their elbow, arm out, like they're balancing a teacup on their heads as they walk. That's the problem with being hip, even some girly thing that's supposed to be nothing more than pure silly girl stuff is just another way of giving a guy a hard-on, making her walk a certain way so her ass sticks out more. So, I have a messenger bag. And that's not giving a hard-on to anybody, believe me I'd know by now. A backpack would at least attract a certain guy, but even I won't do a backpack, even when I was in college I couldn't pass for college-age.

And my face is mousy, it's round but not fat, but it's not slender either. There's nothing fantastic about it, but also nothing ugly. So nobody says anything at all. My eyes are too small for my face, and it doesn't help that I squint even in the shade, and since they're dark like my hair no one can see them, and I've never needed glasses, otherwise that'd be something distinguishing, something I could push up on my nose or adjust or clean with the tail of my shirt, some smooth automatic thing for someone to see, some set of motions to get me noticed, the stretch of my arms or my fingers.

And I'm sure I walk like a boy. I don't think my body is ugly or even unattractive, but I don't know what to do with it. I've never gotten much attention from men, and even the little I have, it's not me walking across a room that they notice. Put it this way, if there's a way of slowly walking with your hands in your pockets and hugging your bag and your jacket close to you, and with your head hanging a bit and then a bit more, and the strides getting smaller and smaller and your steps not going straight ahead anymore so much as in a circle, till you're barely moving and you just spiral out and disappear—that's what I'd wish for, and it probably looks like it.

My fingers feel slender sometimes, but I don't color the nails, and when I brush my hair behind my ears when I'm sitting down, or brush my hair behind my ear as I eat or look at something or read, or when I adjust myself in the chair, switching from one leg crossed under me, ankle to ankle—I feel graceful then, fluid, I feel feminine. I feel like I'm doing something girls or women do. I guess it's gracefulness, really, which is so stupid, if that's what being a woman is in my mind, putting on some effortless show, a woman is only what she's doing smoothly, walking or moving in her clothes or getting up or running her fingers through her hair—that's such bullshit. But that's what it is, to me, how I'm looked at and what I look like parading in front of everyone, even though no one is looking at me.

And since I'm short—squat, really—I can't pretend I have any legs, or slender arms, or a neck worth anything—that is unless I weigh next to nothing, and I don't weigh next to nothing believe me, and since I'm short it's so easy for me to be fat. Every winter my waist and thighs run in and around my stomach and it's all one thing, not a gut and not huge, just a thing, just some shape in the middle of my body that's just blah and nothing, it's so disheartening, you have no idea. But even when I gain weight my boobs don't get any bigger, they're always tiny but I rarely ever wear anything tight so nobody notices that anyway, just great unnoticed short black hair and dark eyes and pants (never a skirt, and hardly ever a dress, and when I do it's got to go down to my ankles for sure) and my clonking big dress shoes, I love my damn polished shoes, they're tremendous.

When I'm at my worst I feel naked even with my fingers out, grabbing at a pen or typing something or holding a phone, I wish I could wear those finger-tip-less gloves all day long. I thank God everyday for clothes, I can't imagine what men think. Or I do, I know. I don't mean what they think of me, that they see my hands or mouth and imagine me specifically, it's just that whatever any man may think of me in passing when he sees my hand or mouth or body—me fucking him or sucking him off or my hands all over him and telling him how good it is, always the quickest and worst thought—I'm sure he'd linger with those thoughts a little longer if someone else were in his general vicinity. I know if I'm seen from the right angle my butt looks pretty good, my back arched when I stand a certain way, there's some sense of proportion and shape, but why I know this or care I don't know.

How men walk around wanting to screw whatever moves

all day long is beyond me. I'm no prude and I'll lose control and become crazy when the moment comes, I'll make love and hardly make a sound and cry afterwards and I'll fuck and yell and say everything, but all that's only after a good while, a good chance, after real words, some real emotion and a lot of playing around, a lot of starting slow or going fast and stopping, a lot of laughter and playfulness and a lot of dead serious emotion and talking. It's men who can have sex without emotion. I know, I know, some women say they can but they're full of it and are just damaged and broken after awhile, acting like they don't care about emotions and connections when that *is* all they care about.

* * *

But I didn't start all this for that. I wasn't going to write any of it down, but I have to now, after what's happened. I wasn't going to write it down because that's how it started, him writing it down and leaving it lying around. It's this guy at my work—I won't use his name, since he at least had the sense not to use her name. That's as much as I'll say, him and her. (And it goes nicely with my refusal to write any brand names down too, there won't be anything here.) I try to keep this space only for me talking about me, but I should try to get all of this out before I forget it. The short of it is I caught him looking at this girl at my work, nothing creepy, not stalking or anything, but it was pretty consistent, kind of strange, and the more I watched him the more I noticed him watching her. But I didn't know that at first, and just one time at lunch I saw he'd dropped a sheet of paper on his way out of where he usually sits at lunchtime, not with everyone else in our building but in a cafeteria nearby. Obviously I go there too, it's quieter and you don't have to see everybody you're staring at all day long. And most of the time she went there too.

It was just part of a sheet of paper torn off, I couldn't read most of what it said, his handwriting is awful, and at the time I didn't think it'd turn into anything major so I didn't really read it, just saw that he'd dropped it. And any normal person would've called out to him as he was walking away, but I'm not that type, I hate to draw attention to myself and the place is usually quiet and I didn't want everyone staring at me, so I just picked it up. He sits near me and when I got back from lunch I said something small like *You dropped this*, and then I probably made a look I didn't realize I was making (I always do that), and I just dropped it on his desk. But his face completely changed, like I'd seen him naked or something. I could tell he was upset. And it even took him like a half hour to even acknowledge it on his desk, I sit like two people behind him and was curious after his reaction and just watched him, and finally he so obviously used moving some crap around as an excuse to snatch the paper up quick and shove it in his pocket. And it was completely none of my business but I suddenly wished I'd looked at the note more closely. All I can remember is that it was a list and one of the things it said was something like *from out of state, or from the country, almost poor, uncomfortable here and in nice clothes.*

And it took me a few days but I realized he was avoiding me, and whatever that note had been was serious, at least to him. It was too bad, since I got along with him real well. If anyone else had dropped something I would've left it there, no way I would've felt comfortable approaching them after lunch with it, but we're both kind of quiet, and the few times we've talked he seems real nice. He's married and I saw him a few times with his wife who works nearby and it's obvious they love each other—and that might sound like some small thing but it isn't, at least to me. Other guys his age who're married all talk about their wives like they're laboring under a nag and a bitch, but he's never talked that way once, not even as a joke. It's true all these other guys' wives probably are bitches—it's the role they've accepted, same as the guys, who have to act stupid and clueless. But he never did any of that, and I respected it. And I could tell he hated talking in front of groups, or walking in front of people who were sitting down. And he's kind of cute, a little fat in the face maybe depending on what he's wearing or what angle you see him from, and he only seems to have one pair of jeans and he never cleans his shoes (it takes him weeks to polish up water damage from walking through puddles, and it annoys me to notice it and wish he'd clean it, since by then the water has damaged the shoes and there're those ripples) and I think he's still got a tiny bit of dandruff, and while he has glasses, throughout all this he's stayed with contacts, I think because he thinks he looks better that way, you can see his eyes real clear, but I'm always partial to guys in glasses. It's something to take off, so the face is something to find, it's romantic, like taking off clothes before you really do. I mean, I don't mean to be a cliché girl myself either, but sex is only great if you have those small things alongside it, like the glasses or the hairs on his knuckles or something, the most explicit things are just dumb body parts without things that seem innocent and unintended, like the vulnerability of black socks fallen down to his shoes on one ankle, but still held up and tight on the other ankle, and you wonder why and watch him fix it, and get a glimpse of his leg hair or his ankle or shin, or when he bends down and the shirtsleeves he's wearing rides up and you see his upper arm is all white, and there's a birthmark or two, or a bulge of a muscle, it's so attractive to see but that's only because they don't know it is and don't try to do it. Anyway.

So we got along real well, and once he said something to me like, *I would never want to be a woman*, and I could tell it was something he'd wanted to say for a long time. I said why and he said because women have to put up with so much bullshit, half the attention we get must just be from schmucks, and how it must be obvious if the guy's just an idiot, but you still have to put up with him, you say something nasty to one but there's just going to be another one. And how a woman doesn't have to do much of anything to get all the attention she wants. And how, generally, men are stronger and bigger than women, so that violence and rape are possible at any time. (He didn't use the word rape, he seemed squeamish to talk to me about sex.) And how women are made to want to love makeup and jewelry and clothes and everything, but how they only want these things by admitting they're ugly or deficient without it. All of this sort of poured out, I'm making him say it like I would, but he never stopped in the middle and said, *I mean you, too,* he never said anything like, *Even though you're not stereotypically pretty, I'm sure you get a lot of unwanted attention.* It was kind of flattering that he didn't qualify everything and wasn't trying to impress me. I know the dumb thing girls always do, where they meet a guy and they say how nice he is because *when he talks to me he's not talking at my boobs,* but if the people who say this are around someone like that long enough, someone who survives on being pretty will actually get annoyed at the guy who's obviously ignoring her tits. They like the idea of this nice man who really wants to talk and listen, but they're not really able to deal with this kind of man, and in some way they don't really want to (it'd be too much of a risk), and that's why they end up the dumb nag who marries the dumb clueless guy: they're not really this way, but they make themselves that way, and so they are. It's sad.

I don't think this is how I was being, I don't think. But I couldn't help having a small crush on him for a few weeks after. He's a little short for me, or I guess just too *like* me, but I know how he smells and I wondered how my smell would be with his, my face and his face, or I would imagine him saying all of what he'd said except in bed, or out somewhere across a table drinking coffee or whatever, where it's just the two of us and we forget what time it is and don't notice the other crowds coming in, or it's so late and the bar crowd shuffles in, and we only notice them when we leave. It was pretty silly. I dreamt about his lips at my ears, and his hands, and I dreamt that the ring on his finger was from me. None of this was serious, it wasn't a big deal, I'm not about to do anything with a married man, he wasn't my best friend or anything, but I did feel real bad when he started to avoid me.

* * *

So I tried to remember what I saw on the note, tried to think of what was on it that would make him so uncomfortable—and also, let's be real, what made him so stupid: if this thing was so hush-hush, how'd he let himself drop it? So I went to the same place for lunch and watched him. He had his laptop with him but he kept opening and closing it, putting his hands over his face, like someone who's tired and confused but just exaggerating it. At some point a girl got up from the table next to his, another girl from our work, and he said something quick to her as she left, and from then on he just read from a book, and didn't seem agitated at all. That didn't say anything to me until a few days later, when I saw him out front of our building in the morning, where it's pretty empty and even a bit cold, but he was just sitting there alone, reading, and looking up constantly. I'd sat outside there in the morning a million times myself and seen him, and I had to admit he always looked distracted while he was reading, always looking up, and I do remember thinking *why doesn't he read somewhere where he can concentrate and not be distracted?*, because everybody who's coming in in the morning is always walking by right where he was sitting, a corner table out in the open.

And then I saw it. That same girl, the one he'd been sitting near at lunch, she walked by in the morning and he stopped what he was doing and watched her go by. I don't think she saw him, but he wasn't doing anything to hide the fact that he'd seen her. And then I remembered the only part of the note I'd seen and could read, *from out of state, or from the country, almost poor, uncomfortable here and in nice clothes.* I didn't know much about this girl, but I was here when she was hired and she was from some more rural area (but not out of state), and so she was a bit poor, or had that look. I mean, she was both of those things, she was the opposite of me: I've never been lower-class or in the country, but I can't dress for shit, I'm not fashionable at all. But she caught on right away and looked spectacular—to me, at least (and apparently to him). To other women they'd probably find something catty and bitchy to say, but whatever. And she was nice. She was always on the phone with her mom or dad about something, and sounded genuinely lovely with them (even though it seemed they were divorced). She's tall (taller than him by a few inches, which always baffled me, if he knew that or what he thought if he did), so I guess that helps with the clothes, slender everything but not starving-looking, so just the right clothes and shoes, a little ring here or a bracelet there, and everything looks flowing and right. I just can't match that look at all. And actually, it wasn't until his note that I noticed that, for as good as she looks and how confidently she acts, sometimes she really did seem uncomfortable in nice clothes, really did seem uncomfortable in an office like ours, or maybe just in the city. I notice people all day long, especially other women (I probably check out other women as much as men, but just to unfavorably compare myself to them) but I never noticed this about her. And so for all that she seemed smart, genuinely emotional, she talked to other people at work, she seemed like a real person for sure. And when I thought about it, if that was all I saw in her, I thought she'd be a good match for him—if he wasn't married, and if she didn't have a boyfriend (which I assumed she did, I thought I heard her talking about him once, and she got picked up by some guy one afternoon).

But there was another part of her that was so dumb and girly, at least to me. Maybe I was just jealous he was noticing her and not me, but on her desk she had all these pictures of babies, and that was it. No pictures of these nice parents she supposedly had, or her on vacation or her out with friends or of a sunset or a sports team or the city skyline or whatever else people have, just of babies, and her with the babies, and her smiling and sitting to the side and always posed the same way, even with the baby, to make herself look as skinny as possible. Turns out the kids are all her sisters' or her cousins' kids, which I didn't know at first. When she was first hired I thought she must be a pretty prodigious single mom—she wasn't wearing a ring, and was mid-twenties like me, and I thought she'd spent the last seven years fucking up with a half dozen guys or more. Thankfully the kids weren't hers at all. But it was obvious she wished they were. Women have really dumb and silly and (since I'm in a sympathetic mood) sad ways of advertising their desire to be mothers. Her desk and her office just screamed, *I'm looking for someone to father my kids.*

* * *

Now that's just being mean. I know that. It's not that negative, I have to be honest with myself. But in my own way I felt attached to him, this guy who'd been with his wife for close to ten years and they didn't have any kids themselves, and I got the sense they'd thought about it and didn't want them, or knew they weren't the type to be parents. And since I feel the same way I was on his side, and I was horrified to think he'd end up with this girl because of her body and how good she looked, only to end up filling her with a bunch of kids and stretching that lovely body out and ruining it and whatever fantasies he's been having with the reality of kids in the next room, and lots of them.

And there I go being mean again. But he just didn't seem

any more the fathering type than I've ever felt myself to be a mother. That's really it. But I don't think it's mean to say that some girls who get out of college and get a real job at a boring place like here are just ticking off things in some mental notebook which ends with finding some schlub and making babies. Women just don't think about it, women's first thoughts are that they can have babies and so they *should*, not what they're going to do with them or how they'd raise them. And yes I know the best parts of love and romance (and so I'm sure about children) is the spontaneous stuff you can't plan for or guess, but some forethought should go into having kids, I would think. And I've thought about it and thought about it, I've agonized about it, I've looked at other women my age who have one or two or three kids, I've looked at women who are twenty and start right then, and are either still married and happy ten years later or who've divorced the guy and are left pulling three kids apart in the meantime. I've questioned my motives and my desires endlessly, I've had make-believe conversations with my make-believe husband about this (so of course he agrees with me!), and I've realized that any desire I have for children comes from the wrong place. I want to have a child and not get divorced like my parents did, I want to have a son or a daughter and be more lenient with some things and stricter about others than my parents were, and both of these are insufficient excuses to procreate.

Or I watch a movie where the husband or the wife dies and the one or the other is left with the kids and there's the scene of them at the dinner table together, barely lit, sad but so intimate and loving, and I want that feeling of me against the world with someone else beside me who depends on me. Or how I miss my growing up, or how I wished I'd gone to this high school or actually gone away to college rather than staying in town, and so much else, it's just embarrassing to put all this down and I hate myself for it, but at least I realized it had nothing to do with creating another life and loving it and caring for it unconditionally and raising it for its own sake, at least I saw it had nothing to do with the idea of it actually growing up and possibly being a completely different person than me.

At least I've realized that. Even though it hurts terribly sometimes, seeing a woman with her baby. So that's why I live alone and have cats. There was a girl in my high school who disappeared after sophomore year, and she'd apparently told someone she was going to have a baby to have something to love, and I saw her years later at a parade with that baby she had so she could have something to love, and she looked miserable. And it's no different than some girl in her mid-twenties who gets dropped by the guy she thought she was going to marry going out and getting knocked-up by some random idiot she doesn't even want around, just so she can be a single mother and love something. It's so strange how we begin to feel that if we aren't married by twenty-five then it'll never happen, how hopeless that begins to feel. It's all so complicated and sad and hard. Like when these women have kids, how they're made to feel stupid and lacking and old and not fun, and these sad mothers in their thirties who can't shove it all out of their peripheral vision, all the magazines and TV shows and gossip that just make them feel like horrible human beings because they're not out and free and unfettered and dressing like a whore or a celebrity. And that's not even getting into what it makes men do. Or it's just some woman who wants to be a mother but is just terrified by the idea, and these confessions come out of them all of a sudden, especially to quiet people like me who attract confessions, and they're perfectly formed speeches, they've just been waiting for someone to listen—they have all these friends but can't tell these friends the most important things, they spend all their time with these friends who actually seem to hate them.

* * *

But I keep forgetting what I'm really writing about here. For whatever reason, and despite my misgivings (as if they matter!) he seemed to attach himself to her. I don't know how long this had been going on, but I watched him from then on and became sure of it. He'd get to work early to sit outside and be all fidgety until she walked by, and then he'd settle down, or go in himself. Up until then he'd be looking all around, everywhere, and then when she passed he'd calm down. Or at our lunch spot, now that I knew to look out for it, he watched her, or watched for her, constantly. He'd be looking around and looking around, and if she didn't show up, he'd get up and leave. But if she showed up, like a light switch he'd stop looking around, and he'd stay.

I couldn't help but think he was frustrated about the whole thing sometimes, that he was falling for someone so unlike him or what he was otherwise interested in. I did some searching around online and found an old blog he and his wife did together and all they talked about were the nerdy and heady movies and music they like, and in one he talked about the books he'd bought for Christmas, and they were just way out there stuff, science and ice age something or another. There's no way she'd care about any of this. And then it'd all spill over into work, and everything he did seemed calculated to be around her if he could, though he rarely ever was. I never saw the two of them talking except once, and that was late. They worked in entirely different departments and so had no reason to see each other. And by this time, whenever he came in looking tired or upset in the morning, it wasn't the weather or a bad commute or a fight with his wife I assumed, but something to do with her. It got to be real silly.

And it struck me at some point that I really had nothing to go on this at all, except his look when I gave him the note back, and what I thought the note said, which could've meant anything about anybody, he could've been having a bad day. He avoided me after that, but that could've all been in my head too. What did any of it mean? What did any of it prove? Here I was, feeling sorry for a nice guy who I imagined was being ignored by some woman who interested him, nearly every time forgetting that he was married, and apparently happily so.

*　*　*

Why do our hearts allow us to be in love with more than one person at once? Why is that even possible? And was that what this even was—love? Do you love someone you've rarely spoken to? That may be how all the old novels worked, but today that sounds ridiculous, but then why? Why is that so far-fetched? Most people meet by random, and they start talking, but before then they're just on the other side of a room, not noticing each other. At some point they do notice each other, and before words are even spoken something in them connects. And what if his looking at her, and my assumption of his inner torment about it, was just one of those nights extended over months and months? And he *was* tormented, he had to be, because he never did anything about it—he would've approached her otherwise, and believe me *everyone* at work would've known about that, but he never even slipped up, except with me and the piece of paper.

*　*　*

And then of course, dumb old me, I take *that* to mean something real and true, that he slipped up with me on purpose, all a smokescreen to get my attention. I think on some level that's what I wish it was. I wish the note had said, *dresses weird, cute, I like talking to her, she's awkward and unapproachable like me, and to everyone else this is alienating, but to me it's endearing, weaknesses and clumsiness.*

This is really it. I wish his attention were on me. I wish I could tell him what I think and talk to him about it. I just wish I was involved in this somehow when I'm really not. I do this all the time and I'm so tired of it. I get attracted to a man because he seems sensitive and like me and I want to hold his hand and actually want him to cry on my shoulder and then I want us to fall in love and be emotional and open for the rest of our lives until we both die together at exactly the same moment.

That sounds ridiculous. Let me try to rephrase it: I'm emotional, and sensitive, and passionate, and intense, and I don't know why a man shouldn't love me for that. I don't understand how someone like me who is so cautious and so aware and so worried about everything she does when interacting with everyone, to be aware and considerate and gentle and kind and decent—why am I the one who's alone, when it's all the assholes and all the inconsiderate and mean and petty and superficial and uncaring and unthoughtful and cruel people who all have someone, and someone they invariably mistreat and end up hating, or being hated by? All I see around me are lonely people, the lonely young and the lonely old, at work and on the bus and at lunch and walking around and in the next apartment and car and walking down the street. I feel sometimes like I'm the only person who sees this, and I see it because I'm one of them, but instead of feeling cynical and pushing people away what I actually see is that all of my loneliness and youthful hatred for everything has been washed out of me, and what's left is the real desire to help and to be good and to talk to people who really want to talk. I feel my best self is the one sitting across from one other human being and spilling myself out for him to see, what I mean is just honesty, unabashed and total and complete, and how he would do the same when he saw how honest and total and unafraid I was being. I see fear and hate it and I want to tell that person to stop being afraid.

I know I can do so much good and be so good for someone but it never happens to me, it never happens, and no one I meet seems ready or right for that, I push all the guys away and I have for years now, I was sure I'd be single at least until I was thirty but now I assume forty or fifty, and in the meantime I want to do so much with what I'm filled up with, I want to share and give and offer and just exhaust myself with another human being, but everyone has their friends and their cliques, they have their distractions and their interests that aren't mine, they have their schedules and their reputations or they just look at me as a little mousy girl who's a little ugly and boyish and at first I probably seem unapproachable and I turn away from people and there's a darkness in my face and my eyes and it must just put people off and so nothing happens.

What it really is, is that at this rate no one will ever know me, and that hurts so much, that's just a vacuum cleaning me out, that I'm full for no reason and I'd be empty for no reason. No one will ever know the actual me, the real me, the me deep-down, the me that would be good for them, or the me that needs the actual and real and deep-down him, that wants to be held and wanted and needed and helped and listened to and spoken to. There's a fullness in the middle of my chest that my body doesn't show, my sloppy body all the exercise in the world won't fix.

And why do I still expect things? Where did we get this notion about things we should expect? And so should I expect, or feel I deserve, or should I even want, a real companion? Is there some other priority I'm missing, that when I find it I'll feel so stupid for wanting love in all its ways, emotional and mental and physical and intellectual? Am I just so selfish as all of that, am I so pre-determined by the society outside me that I hate, that I've been told a girl should want love and some prince charming shithead and all the rest, all those false dumb emotions we get from movies and TV? Is that all this really is? All this while I adore him because he is so obviously done under and terrified and torn apart and unable to hide the fact that he's tormented by the real and true emotions he feels, not the fake ones everyone's always making drama about, that he feels real things and sees them as real things and hesitates and is frightened just like me, about these real and true and awful things, awe-filled and wonderful and awful and terrible?

I'm so flawed and buried under, and I don't understand why he didn't look at me instead, I feel terrible to admit this, to have pretended from the start this was any different, like I could write it as a different story, but I would've accepted his advances, people have happy second marriages all the time. And when I see what he wears every week I imagine the closet with those clothes, I imagine my cats getting their hair all over his clothes, I imagine him giving a shit about me and how terrifying it is to be alive and alone.

And once on a Friday, despite himself, this long before all of this happened, he told me he didn't know how he'd ever do his job if he didn't have his wife waiting for him afterwards, that he could go down the elevator and down the street to meet her, and they could go home together, holding hands like I saw them doing, or his hand on her back or up the back of her neck and under her hair, his hand enveloped by her short hair, short like mine only brown, and of course she has glasses, and how she smiled and pulled him close. And after he said that he stopped as if he'd seen the look on my face, as if he suddenly realized that I actually *was* single and actually *did* go down the same elevator and out the same doors to my place, all alone.

And I think that night was the first time I cried over not having him, that he even noticed the change of emotion and hurt on my face or in my posture, that he noticed anything of my face or body and interpreted it so exactly right and immediately crumpled and apologized, and I dreamt of his face all that weekend, and it's just never stopped, and he's not even that good looking, not even that charming, he tells the stupidest most obvious jokes, he's such a boy, and he should've had braces as a teenager but he didn't so his teeth are all crooked, and all of this should make him ridiculous to me, unlovable, even hated, I want to stop feeling for him but I can't, and after what I did I can't even go back to work, I already quit anyway.

And the way he looks at her crushes me, and it's not the same way he looks at his wife because there's also guilt there and the explosion of anguish in the back of his head that I know is there, his uncertainty and hurt over what he feels, being torn. And I've overheard her talk, and probably even talked to her myself, and I've heard her say a million things about guys, how she's dating guys but they never work out, or how she's out at company parties and just starts crying that nobody loves her or that some certain guy she wants doesn't love her anymore, or how she reassures herself with her face piled on with makeup and her super high-heels and the tiny Monday or Thursday purse that matches whatever the fuck she's wearing those days and the sunglasses that would look ridiculous on anyone but her but with her make her look even more beautiful and it's astonishing and I don't blame him at all for looking—but then if you stand real close to her and look at her face, she seems so sad and hurt a million times over and the smoothness of her face at a distance is actually something worn and ragged and I feel sorry for her because she also can't hide her emotions, and I've heard her and women like her say the same boring shit to reassure themselves, that *The wait is worth it*, and *You're still single because you haven't settled and a woman should never settle*, and *You should take big risks because those are the only ones worth taking*, all these empty platitudes that don't mean anything, because I took a big risk and what good did it do me? I wrote him a note, one I'll be happy to forget the contents of, where I essentially told him it was me he loved, or could love, or should love, not her, and not even his wife. Can you believe that? And I cleared my stuff out the same day, told them I was leaving for a rival firm, and there's no quicker way for them to get you out the door than to do that—even though it's a lie and I just needed to leave. And I passed him on the way out and somehow left it for him and somehow even smiled when I turned to say goodbye—and him, weird hair and scuffed shoes and wearing his glasses for once, looking brilliant and boyish and adorable for being completely unaware of what I was talking about, why I was smiling, and what I wished I meant to him.

And today was a week, and I haven't heard a thing because I know I won't, I never do hear a thing, not even a negative word, I just spiral out and disappear like I've secretly always wanted to do. And isn't that grand, to be invisible. And I went down to where I used to watch him eat lunch and watch her, and the place is split up with glass partitions between every three or four rows of tables, so someone could be only a table away but separated by that glass. And I went and sat on the other side of where he was, and of course he was fidgeting and looking around for her and didn't notice me at all, and didn't notice me until he stood up to go and I stood up in unison with him, and that synchronized movement caught his attention out of the corner of his eye, as if the glass had turned into a mirror and he saw the same movement opposite him, and I saw him look over at me, and start at my feet—but go no higher. And he knew me from my shoes! He knew me from my pants—and he wouldn't look any higher, and that great weight in my chest and all that I've ever felt just got caught all in my throat, and it flushed my face and it warmed my entire body, and I even smiled at this moment of his total rejection of me, I smiled because I knew he recognized me from my shoes, that he knew me from that much, that we were that close, at least. And being who he is, he couldn't ignore me or face me but only walked slow, slowly, down the aisle, and I followed his clumsy walk in unison, he never looking at me and me never looking away, until we reached the end of the glass and, despite all those around who I thought might look, I held out my arm and extended my hand as he turned away from me finally.

Games Old Men Play

MY WIFE, SHE WAS THE MUSIC PERSON. SHE LISTENED WHILE SHE COOKED, I couldn't stand it. I don't know German or Italian—I fought them when I was twenty why do I want to understand their language? (Never thought I'd spend my old age listening to people singing—I said screaming—in German and Italian) Anyway, what can you do.

She died, and I had to move to a smaller place, and I didn't want her records, and no young people I know listened to any of that music, you know. I donated them at least. I went back to that store to buy some clothes, and the records weren't there anymore, someone had bought them, I felt good, she would like that.

And I thought that was it. But then I was watching a movie at home (I won't go out to those theaters), and it just reminded me of her, you see, the music. I waited through all the credits to see what it was, all for a damn German name.

Well, I went down to the electronics store the next day. The kid looked terrified when I walked toward him—

nobody was going to approach me, I know how old people are. Sometimes I put on a cute old man act too, slightly clueless, still with a bit of wit, and you get better service, people fawn all over you. But not then, I got it right out of the way, I said straight off, I said where's a good but not too expensive stereo, nothing fancy, I've got a small place, I don't want to play all that thumping garbage.

And I got a little thing for fifty bucks, what the hell else more do I need?

Then I asked him about music, you know, I talked to him about the Wagner. And he showed me where all the operas were, and I was amazed. Now my wife, she listened while she was cooking, all day on Saturday, but I never imagined it was one long opera she was listening to, but these things were five hours, one thing was four of those put together. And they were expensive. I said wait a second, these are almost as much as the stereo. I'm not poor, but that's a lot of money, you see. (And I have to say I was feeling silly, you know—I'm not impulsive, but here I am, I heard music my wife loved and the next day I'm spending fifty dollars to hear it again, it might just be ridiculous.)

Well, he was nice to me. He said go to the library. He said, they might not have the most recent or the best recordings of these things, but they'll have something. I said what's the difference, I just want to listen to them, you know. He said go to the library. So I did. And he was right. The boxes the things came in did look all chewed up, the booklets had no covers anymore—but what do I care, I'm not going to read the book. I doubt she knew everything they were saying, it was the music.

And I put on my little act, there was a line of people and I acted a little confused, and in no time I had a library card and the music CDs, it was the one she liked and the one in the movie, that love story, *Tristan and Isolde*. And I even go back there now in the mornings you see—all the old farts go to the library, they have all the newspapers there, some of the guys won't take their coddling, they act all grouchy. Why bother with that, you know? The sign says no drinks or food in the library, but after a few minutes of me acting a little slow, and they're all, okay old man, don't worry about it, and I have my breakfast sandwich and coffee and a newspaper in the library.

Anyway, you know, I took the stereo and the CDs home. I set it all up by the kitchen and near the couch. My fingers even got those tiny little batteries into the remote control. And I put her picture by the stereo and put on the music. And you know what, I couldn't believe it. I remember records as a younger man, they never sounded like this. It was even better than in the movie, since there was no movie sounds blocking it all up. I listened to it all night, and wouldn't you know, I did read the booklet, I read the whole thing and followed it, and her picture was right by me the whole time. Made me sad I never listened with her.

The next morning I went to the bank to see how much

money I had, and I returned the stereo for one twice as much. Because, you only live once. I saw the same young man, I said to him, I said thank you, I said he made an old man really happy. And all my neighbors that day, all the other guys who wouldn't dream of this, the same ones who don't even drive anymore and just *sit* there all day, what do they hear but me, they hear me and that's right, I can still move, I rearranged the entire living room to put this thing in. Moved it all around, I was shirtless and down to my sweat-shorts, I didn't need anybody's help, I felt fit, the blood pumping, all that.

And I sat and listened to the opera again. Those poor kids! It doesn't seem anything like that is possible anymore, that two people would kill each other because they couldn't be together. I remember how her father didn't want her marrying me, but we married anyway, we were married fifty years, people make up their own mind now, you see. If they love each other, they get married. Now the kids in the opera, they had responsibility to their kings and whatnot— we don't have kings anymore, and if rich people still have marriages like that to hell with them, let them ruin their kids. Still, you see, when the girl mourned over the boy, I heard how I was at my wife's grave. I couldn't cry or say anything about it, but that's how I felt, I never thought I'd hear how I felt from some lady singing in German that's for sure, but I got over the surprise pretty quick, there was nothing like it.

I tried to explain this to some of the other guys on my floor, they didn't want to hear about it, they just wanted to see the stereo. They were impressed I figured out how to use it, and then I showed them how to. The readout on the thing was even bigger than on the first one, the buttons on the remote control were big too, even for all our shaking. They said why am I listening to this German crap, they wanted all the jazz from when we were younger. They had that at the library too—and if they didn't, they said they could get it from somewhere—all the singers too, big bands, and so I ended up having a dozen old men in my place, we played cards and had cigars and bullshitted, you see.

Even had to put up with the sound of men in my bathroom. I stopped going to public bathrooms God, ages ago, when she was still alive, I'd gotten too old to hear other men rushing into a stall all huffing and hearing their zipper and their plop down onto the seat and all the damn groaning from their mouths and all the spluttering besides—men are sick. And now it was all back in my place. We were crude and young again. You know. We all commented when we heard noises, and one said it's good at least he's not jerking off in there, and the rest say as if he could anyway, ha-ha. We even drank a bit, but we can't do too much of that anymore. Made me think of how many more old men I could've had over, if they hadn't died back there.

That made me sad, you see. I was nobody special, if I was anybody I was just her husband—and she'd hit me on the head and say that was special enough. She'd be right, anyway. But there were lots of husbands who died, boys who never got to be husbands who died, lots of bastards who lived and will probably outlive me. So I thought that well, I'm still alive, so I tried to talk to the old men at the library more, the grouchy ones, and I tried not to do the cute old man crap anymore. I thought, people died and I'm playing games, that's not right. I hate the fast food place but I started eating my breakfast there instead of the library, I knew some kid there had to wipe off the table at the library when I was done with it and left, I'm sure there were grease spots and he shouldn't have to do that, you see. Then I said, I hate the fast food place, but I get free rides anywhere, my place here has a bus, and I have them take me to a proper restaurant now, a little bit away from the library. I eat there and talk to people I never knew before, and I walk all full and good to the library, and look at the papers. (It might not be a good idea to take that walk in the winter, but you see it means so much that I'm willing to try it, to just say it.) Sometimes I wish she were with me, to see what I'm doing now, but that's a lot of nonsense—if she were here I wouldn't be feeling sad, wouldn't be doing any of these things, I would just be happy with her at home. These are just games old men play to not be alone. The music, the other guys, the stereo, you see—that's all to replace her. I make sure to never forget that.

Because I got burned out by it, it felt silly. I went awhile not listening to anything, I went back to trying to be how

I was before, where I just thought about her. And when I went to the library and got that first opera out, the two kids who are in love, and I came home and listened, it was with just the headphones on, I didn't want anyone to hear. They always came knocking when the music was loud.

It was just the music and me and her picture, you see. And I took the booklet out and went to follow it, like I was reading it to her—when a piece of paper fell from the booklet. It was a due slip from the library. Someone had taken this out in June, just two months ago. I held the note closer to my face and called out her name—the one who'd taken it out had my wife's first name.

I was stunned, you know, and I felt things in me that I hadn't for years. When we knew she was going to die, I watched her and it was slow and mostly painless and we could just hold each other nights and remember. She would say she wouldn't be mad if I got married again. I knew half what she meant—I could marry another woman, you see, but she'd been my real wife, I'd never want to be buried next to anybody but her. She was the woman who had my children, the one I learned to be a man and a husband and a father because of. Another woman at my age would really just be a half thing, you know, our bodies not working, not that great way we had when we were thirty. So what she meant was (she never had to be stern or say too much, I knew what she meant right away), she meant it was okay to pretend, it was better than being lonely.

Because I felt guilty. I did. I have since I saw the slip. I have since I looked up the woman's name in the phone book—her name was right there. I asked the driver of our bus about the street, about how far away it was. I played the cute old man and got those kids at the library to help me with the map thing on the internet. I never gave them the address, just the street. I could see the apartment building where she lived, I could see the door she went in when she came home with the CDs.

I finally did call the number and ask for her. It felt like I was fifteen. A young man answered on the third ring and I asked for her, and he said no, she's at work, and he gave the name of the place, a bar. I was too nervous and just said no, don't worry, I acted like I was from the library and said some books had come in for her. He said sorry, said I sounded like one of her friends.

Well, that was a few hours ago, and I've done the whole deal, shit shave and shower. I've got a hundred dollars in my pocket. Last job I had, an indoor sports place nearby where I went three times a week and filled the pop machines, I would tell the young kids there, I would say, I said to always have fifty bucks in your pocket, you don't know what will happen. And I'll have twice that. I won't get all dressed up, that bar's nothing fancy, I don't want to stick out. I just want it to seem normal. If I sounded like one of her friends, she must be younger than me by only a bit—and if she's still working at a bar, I don't remember hearing anything but young people going to that bar, but maybe it's changed. And the young man must be her son. I don't know what he would be doing at her place—she couldn't be young enough to still have children living with her. Maybe a grandson, he could've been a teenager.

Anyhow, the bus is here. I tell the driver to drop me at the church, and to pick me up there in four hours. There's something going on there I can pretend I'm going to, you see. And if she drives a car, I can call the bus and not have them come to get me. I feel nervous, coming into the downtown, it's just getting dark. I don't know how I'll bring up the opera, how I'll talk, or try to. With my wife, I just brought things up, you know, if I wanted to talk to her about something, I just did it. Or she did. I haven't needed to talk to another woman like this for half a century, and I laugh at this to myself, and the driver looks at me funny, looks at me like I'm senile. I never thought I'd be so old.

Off the bus, suddenly I want a cigarette. I go to a store on the corner and get a pack and some matches, right near the bar. The kid starts to ask for my ID and then laughs. Outside, the bar's old electric sign is just across the street. I'm afraid she'll come out just now and leave, so I run across even though the traffic coming this way is far down the street, no reason to run but I feel good, I feel so much better, to be out.

The bar is mostly empty, it's only a weekday, you see. The ones at the bar or the ones at the jukebox or the ones in the corner, I bet they're always here, they get to see her every night, they're very lucky. I'm glad no one's playing any music yet, I can't stand new music. There's only some sports show on from two TVs above the bar. That jog across the road took something out of me, it takes a few seconds to climb up onto a stool, to find the footrest so my legs don't dangle and ache. My elbows are on the bar, and a cook goes by with his turned-around hat and a bad shave—there's someone who talks to her all the time, another one. And there's a guy bartender but he's talking to somebody down there, and a girl comes through some double-doors after the cook went in, and someone down past me says her name—

Is that right? *That's* her? She's younger than my daughter, can't be thirty. *Christ's sake.* And dressed—how do you dress like that? Nothing for a man to wonder at, no mystery at all, it's no worse than movies, but I don't come around places like this often, and this's why, you see. But I can't keep from staring at her face, her hair, she walks wonderfully, it was a body like this my wife had after the war—I mean she never showed it off in public and got men drinks, but I remember a body like this. And her face, the way she talks to the man who called down to her, she's so kind, I wonder if I've ever seen anyone more kind. And she likes the opera, somehow she likes the opera, I think of her leaving this place at night and going home and listening to it, or in her car.

She comes to me and asks me what I want. I don't know what to say. I say just a soda, for now—and I say for her not to call me sir, she just called me sir, and she says she's always been taught to respect her elders, and I steam inside and I keep myself from saying the cute old man remark, and this comes out, "Give the old your pity, not your respect." She laughs because it came out strange, and she comes back with a drink. I can't sound angry, not to her—even that worst thing sounded ridiculous and cute, she even refills it and says not to worry about it, even pity isn't something just about money.

I finally order something real and tell her to start me a tab, I want to show her I have the money. I sit and drink but can't get her attention, people her age are just too much, I've picked the wrong day to come and after eight some hockey game comes on and a bunch of kids from the college come in, they bump into me and are loud, they put the music on from the jukebox, they scream at each other since they can't talk at a normal voice. And they all smell, the men all smell of terrible cologne, they're dressed in torn jeans and these shirts with designs on them that are made to look old, but aren't. These are the ones she likes, or the ones maybe *has* to like, she's just a bartender, doing her job—but who'm I kidding, she *does* like them, she doesn't listen to any of that opera music herself, it must be some project, she must still be in school—is it possible she's that young?

Pathetic. I can't get her attention anyhow. I leave the cigarettes on the bar and a few bills on the counter and *shit*—I'm fine, *I'm fine*, almost fell into a group of these smelly men, these boys, they're all just fucking boys these days, that barstool and the few drinks did that, they say stupid things, call me grandpa and old man, they say I'm hammered, but I'd killed men and seen horrendous suffering before I was their age, I had to reconcile myself to all of that, and all they have to do is waste their money on clothes and doll up like a woman and put their hair in spikes and they're just sick.

Outside at least, it's much quieter. I shouldn't have come here, you know, I know that now. A first name is nothing, if I'd died first I can't imagine my wife hankering after a stranger who has my name. She would feel foolish at the thought, and I feel foolish now. I always told her, I said it when we were courting and I made a dumb mistake, I told her that I don't see something as stupid, until I do it. I haven't changed in fifty years. I miss her so much.

My hands are on my knees and I cough until it hurts, all that smoke and shit in my body again, no reason for it. I stand up and try to breathe slowly, there's still two hours until the bus comes back, I don't want to call it early. I just want to stand here, get the smell of smoke off me.

Two people come out of the bar. She's one of them. The man starts to talk, he's the one I heard on the phone, he's one of those perfumed men, how long does it take for these men to get dressed? I don't know what they're saying, I think they've been fighting, that's how she's talking to him. Men are so foolish, they want all the wrong things. And women comply. He just wants to kiss her again and they go back and forth and now they are kissing, that kind of kiss only the young are capable of, as if they never have kissed but are scared they never will again, as if a kiss covers up whatever it is that's bitter between them. As if the bodies they have now, are enough to have. I know how they feel.

I shift my feet on the sidewalk and they pull apart and see me in the dark. They're embarrassed at first, but when I don't look away—I won't look away, I refuse to look away—they're all offended, like I'm disgusting, like I just want to leer at them. I can't say anything. They mutter something and go back inside. I'm too old to do anything but be muttered at. I wish the man would fight me.

I hate them. I hate that I was moved by a movie to remember my wife. My wife wasn't a movie. My wife wasn't her cooking music on a Saturday. I don't know what my wife was, except that she's gone.

I walk further on, and this is just how things are, you see, all the crowded bars and the street with its shops, and not five minutes of walking for an old man and there's an old trainyard. Either no boxcars anymore, or rusted ones, black boxes. And then behind it is the river in August, and on the other side of the river, hills and houses. No more farmland from when I was little. And if I did see that farmland, there would still just be houses with lights flickering, whole rooms lit with flickering light, movies and things not to remember. It wasn't always like this. I stand here for a long time.

I come back near the church and find the bus is there early. It's dark and the driver doesn't see me coming, I see him rush off the bus and run into an alley, the run of a man who must piss immediately. I approach the bus, only a small thing, really a shuttle—that's right, that's what they call it, a shuttle, ten seats, maybe fifteen, and a step up to get there. It's locked, but its entire inside is lit up with that awful yellow light, unnatural, like a room somebody just made in the middle of the street, and there are windows all around it and seats you aren't supposed to be comfortable in, and that light makes me squint to be inside. It's locked and I can't get in until the driver returns, but it is empty and waiting, just for me.

Adult Conversation

I'M GLAD THEY DIDN'T LET ME SIT IN THE FRONT SEAT FOR MY BIRTHDAY. I never like the front seat. Dad and mom are always driving, and then I can't see out those windows. I sit in the middle in the back so then I look anywhere. And in the front seat everything is faster going by. In the back seat I can turn and then watch and then things are slower. I can see people better too. I can get up on my knees and—

"Sit down honey," mom is saying, "put your seatbelt on."

"But it's my birthday."

"Why don't we let you sit on the train tracks because it's your birthday too."

"Okay!"

Dad says my name. "Come on." I listen to dad better. "And sit on one side or the other. You're getting too big to sit in the middle."

"Really?"

"When you're sitting on your knees looking out the back window, yes."

I get off my legs and then scooch over behind dad's seat. He's driving today. I see his face in the middle mirror because I know what happens. He has his driving face and then he sees me see him and then he makes a weird face and then I laugh.

"What?" mom is saying, like I did something bad.

"Nothing," dad is saying.

Mom doesn't understand, I make jokes with dad more than I make jokes with mom. But she makes a face now like she's left out and I don't like that. I want to make her feel better and say, "We almost there?"

"Almost, honey. A few minutes. You've been there before."

I know that, I always come here on my birthday. But I feel like I've been in the car for forever. I see all the other restaurants we go by but none of them are where we're going. That one there is where they got busted for having bugs in the food. That's gross, but I wish I could've seen it.

But my belly grumbles. But at least we're driving finally. Mom was in the grocery store for forever. Sometimes I'm so hungry that I think that if I wait too long then I won't be able to eat, because then I'll be nervous too much. And we're going to the baseball game after we eat! I want to be able to eat because I know we can't get a lot of food at the baseball game, I know what mom and dad can afford. I don't want to make them mad at me asking about too many hot dogs.

And the waitress girls will be at the restaurant. They always look at me when they know it's my birthday, one of them messed up my hair and then tugged on my ear once, then I didn't know what to do. Even dad laughed then, and I got nervous. I liked it better when I didn't know they were pretty, they were just older then, now I know they're older than me but not as old as mom and dad, and then I get nervous. I remember when I first started to feel that way, about the gym teacher at school, since she's the only teacher who doesn't have to wear all those clothes, and then we were glad the nuns aren't our gym teacher, that would be gross—

We're here! I always think I remember how things look, and then it's always better. Sometimes there's too many people and then we have to wait and we sit by the door all the way inside where there's a big table and a bunch of newspapers on it, and the car magazines. I love the car magazines, I'm always looking at the cars. But then if they had a magazine for those big machines, ones for the big trucks with the shovels and the flatteners that remake the parking lots, I would look at those first, but they don't make magazines for those, I've never seen them. I took my bike once to the school parking lot when they were doing that and it stayed there all day.

And next to the door is always the big tall ashtray, it's all silver and has a big hole on the top. I keep thinking it's like where the Holy Water is in church but I know that's silly. They don't let people smoke cigarettes around here anymore, but somebody wants to keep the ash tray. And if it's really too many people we stay in the hallway, and then there's a board there with signs on it and pictures, but it's boring stuff, people who want to cut your lawn or who lost their cats, I hate cats.

But they're going to put us in our seats right away, mom and dad did that on purpose, they said we should get here early, and that worked. The waitress girl has red hair and she smiles at me and I want them to tell her it's my birthday. And they do! And she puts her hands on her legs and gives me the menus and then tells me to lead the way, and then she even says I can sit anywhere. I look down one place but there's a bunch of old ladies sitting there, and they remind me of the old ladies that are in the church when I'm in the church in the morning and serving mass. They're always sitting in the dark with their rosaries and they always scare me, and I don't want to sit by them. But I don't want to turn around and look dumb or make mom and dad think I'm dumb so I go to a table where I can just not face them, but I know I'll still think they're looking at me, like in a scary movie when people are looking at you.

I play around with the tablecloth because it's plasticy on top, but it's where somebody's tore it and it looks like little pieces of cotton are falling out. When I don't think mom and dad are looking I like to put my fork in there and then make the hole bigger.

Mom and dad get their coffees and then I get my pop and then they bring the bread too, and if you eat all the bread then they bring you more. The butter is always melty and I put it on the bread like I'm coloring to the end of the lines, so the whole bread is covered with the butter. And then I take a bit and then I drink the pop and then it's like the bread melts.

And if I'm chewing when the waitress girl is around I swallow real fast because I don't want to have my mouth full when I order. Mom and dad just let me start doing my own ordering, and I want to do it right. And I point on the menu where the cavatelli is, and then I make sure to say the word real slow otherwise I can't say it, and then I tell her that I want applesauce and not salad. Mom and dad always get salad, and it feels funny to be disagreeing with them about that, but they've never talked about it. I just like the applesauce better.

Now is when mom and dad start talking together. Dad always sits back in his chair and then he puts his arm on the empty chair on the other side of me, and then he holds his coffee cup. When he does that I know they're about to start talking, and that's usually after we order the food.

They talk about adult things, and then I try to do something so I can listen but they don't know I'll listen. I sip water from my little water glass and hold it in my straw with my finger and then drip it on the tablecloth, since on this one it stays there like a bubble and slides around, and when I do it at home on mom's tablecloth is sinks into it and leaves a wet spot, but it never does that here, it's a different kind.

And then I think of my brother, he doesn't like going out to eat with mom and dad, and now he's old enough to stay at home and doesn't have to come out all the time. I think even when I get old enough I'll still go out to eat with them, it feels like I have them to just me, or like I'm an adult. They talk about adult things at home, but when we're out and I'm with them it feels like something else—

Oh—and I take my birthday money out and then count it a few times. I had mom take it to the bank and then make them all singles, so it looks like I really have a lot. And then I take mom's pen from her purse and a piece of paper. Because grandma gave me twenty dollars last year, I know that because I wrote it, but this year she gave me thirty-five dollars, and I try and figure out how much I'll get in five years, and six—

And right then mom starts talking about grandma, and I always feel weird when they start talking about somebody I'm thinking about, it's like they know.

"Oh mama still won't believe it," mom is saying, and it's weird to hear her call someone mom.

"What about grandma?" I say. I know she means her mom since dad's mom died before I was around.

"Oh nothing honey."

"Well she's blind if she can't see what's going on," dad is saying.

"She's just old—"

"She has to know by now that there are bad politicians, bad cops, bad whoever. And there are bad priests, too."

I don't want to listen. I know it's something. Because when I serve mass people made jokes about that, the older boys mostly. I don't understand what they mean but they say it like how they make fun of people, it's something they laugh at me about. And it's probably about sex, they have that look too.

"I tell you," dad is saying, "if anyone—I don't care who it was—ever touched our boys, I swear I'd kill them, I don't care if I went to jail—"

"Honey—"

"Well I would—"

He has his hand on the seat across from me and I'm glad I'm not sitting on his side today. I don't know what's wrong with a touch, but then I don't want to ask, dad's face is red. He gets mad about hitting, I don't know why about touching though. It must be bad because dad said he would kill him. I try to imagine that, like the movies, dad with a baseball bat or a gun hitting someone or shooting them, or then like that dad in the movie with an ax in the snow, and the kid my age running away from him.

Dad's not like that! He gets angry and spanks us, and

then one time he got mad at my brother while mom was driving and then grabbed him in the back seat and that made me cry, but that's not killing, killing is bloody, but I still cried in the car when it happened. I felt silly for crying but I couldn't help it, it just happened and it made me cry.

Now the waitress girl has the food and I eat a bunch, but then I just watch dad's knife and his fork, I think of him stabbing someone, or even hitting mom or me. When I was really little and I got my first bike I rode down the street where the two girls were in my class, they were playing in their driveway and then I wanted to make them see me do something, and then there were old people next door to them sitting out on their porch so then I yelled all these swears at them. That was as mad as dad ever got at me.

And mom told me to go say I was sorry later, and she meant say sorry to dad, and when I went and saw him he was sitting upstairs by himself in his chair, and he had put all the lights off, and then I was going to say I was sorry but instead I said if he was okay, and then he just put me in his lap and said he was fine, but then he wouldn't talk any more.

I never try to think about that, he scared me sitting in the chair, it was worse than the spanks since I know I deserved them. I don't want to see him like that anymore.

I think I should quit being an altar boy just in case. Because of dad and because of the older boys. I won't want dad to go to jail for anything, and I don't like being made fun of. But I don't know.

If there's something dad would kill someone else for doing, is there something he'd hurt me for doing, worse than spanking, something I don't know about?

I don't play with the fork and the tablecloth after we're done eating. I try not to cough at all, even when I drink my pop too quick, I don't want to upset him.

When we're done dad goes to the car by himself and then mom says she'll pay the check, and then I ask if I can stay with her, and then I ask if I can put the tip back on the table. I don't want to be alone in the car with him, not right now.

I wait by the boards with the lawn cutting and lost cat things for mom to get out of the bathroom, and then we go to the car together. When we get in the car I sit behind mom instead.

Alone

FRESHMAN YEAR, THIS KID I PLAYED BASEBALL WITH IN THE SUMMERS, HE bets me who'll win a football game on Sunday, says he bets me five bucks, and on Sunday his team wins—

And that whole Monday, I don't have any money in my pockets, I'm scared and waiting for him to show up, wanting his fucking five dollars—

Of course he never does, I'm just an idiot—

People talk and don't know what they say, I listen and I want them to listen to me and know what I say as much as I notice them, nobody does—

Or same year, a kid a year older than me, but we look alike, people say we're brothers, and I can't tell if he's annoyed by this, but we both come in one day with the same haircut just about, and I'm terrified he'll mention it, or that he sees it but doesn't mention it, just hates me—

I'm such an actor, so fake—

I can't stop acting—

I'm just nobody—

When I was little, I would stand in front of my window while I was changing, and I'd flick people off, flick them off just in case there was somebody I couldn't see who was watching me—

A fucking eight-year-old, doing that, there's something wrong with that—

I've never been able to not feel like I'm being watched, ever—

And my room was on the upstairs, I still imagined people, floating there, watching me—

I never closed the shade—

It wasn't that I could hide myself, it was there was always someone there—

I hate myself, that part of myself, I can't get it off me—

I have no idea how I look to other people, I feel hunched over—

The paranoia's worse and worse, until this is just who I am now, I'm constantly nervous around anyone and doing anything—

Well maybe not *constantly*, meaning all the time, seventy-five percent of the time for sure though—

I never feel totally comfortable, which is why I can't tell anyone any of this, I can't even write it, I'm a coward—

Fucking actor—

Nobody—

Alone—

Can't even say it right, how would I even put it—

I can't take anything that talks back, I can't take anything that just listens—

I can't take anything, I hate myself, there's no reason I should be like this, nobody's watching me but I know they are—

I don't think the world's horrible, I'm not like those kids who pretend to be deep, the ones as afraid as me who act like intellectuals, all they do is talk and talk, it all boils down to how awful the world is, what a pile of shit—

I mean I *do* hate everybody, they're as fake as me but they like it, but I don't see the point of talking about it, like it's a mystery or something you fix, the sun comes up in the morning and I hate everyone, so what, that's not a philosophy, wish I could make a list of rules from that but I can't.

* * *

It's just bullshit, the dumbest bullshit, in the lunchroom with like three hundred other kids, freshman to senior, even some kids walking past from the fucking junior high, and passing through the lunchroom are football players who've just worked out, and I see their legs or their arms, and I think everyone else does too, and I think they're just comparing me to them, three hundred kids in the lunchroom and it's me their comparing them to, *Look at him, his legs are shit, his arms are shit, how can he stand to be in here—*

It's not violence, they're not going to come and beat me up, I see the kids who get beat up, I'm definitely not them, at least it's not that—

It's a look, it's what's going on in their heads I can't figure out, that I'm sure is about how ugly I am, how quiet, how stupid—

And there're other juniors, there're even seniors—even teachers, fucking teachers!—who're smaller than me, skinnier than me, or fatter—and the kids from the junior high, how bad must they feel, do they all think this way—

They can't, I'm obviously the only one—

Imagine the world if everyone thought like this all the time, maybe they do, maybe that explains everything—

And if they do I don't know about it, it doesn't matter anyway—

I'm such a—I'm such a fuck, such an actor, so fake, I'm all those, if I could think of more I would and they'd all be true—

Alone—

I can't even put this right, there's no way to talk about it, I don't even make sense to myself—

* * *

I think people notice how I've worn the same pair of pants all week, or how I wore the same shirt two Wednesdays in a row, I assume they notice it, but then I realize

I've never looked at anybody's pants, I don't pay attention to what people are wearing—

Unless it's girls and it's something tight, it's hard to not notice that—

I think it'll get better, I think it will if I give them what they want, what I think they want, make sure they're happy with me—

I don't like it when people are angry with me, all I do is avoid arguments, I don't want to know anybody's opinion of me—

But I do, that's the problem, I so do—

And some people that're sort of like me, they're lucky, they're quiet like I am but they absorb people, they're sponges, they can't talk about it but they can get people's emotions, they can figure people out, they have a way of knowing people, they can trick them in a way, they can predict what people'll do, I've seen it—

I've seen people when they see somebody kissing up to a teacher, coming on to somebody, they smile, and then I notice it too—

It's like you've caught them acting, it's like you pulled their mask off, it's all an act, you smile at it when you see it, a guy trying to pick up a girl—

A guy's always trying to pick up a girl, when's a guy not trying to fucking pick up a girl—

I'd die to be able to do that, to be nosy, to have that advantage, to see what other people can't see about themselves, but all I can see is what I'm not, or what I am, just shit, scared, terrified, can't even talk or explain anything.

* * *

A girl in study hall with big beautiful eyes and a weird smile because of her braces but she's gorgeous, but I don't look at her because I know someone will see me looking at her, or she will, I just want to look at her—

I mean obviously I do because I know that much about how she looks, but I want to look more, I want to just look at her for days and days—

I even sat with a girl once at a basketball game, I was stunned with all these people around that she sat next to me, wanted to talk to me, but it was nonsense, I couldn't talk to her for more than a minute, all I could see were everyone else's eyes on me, everybody was whispering to everybody else, *He's sitting with a girl, look at that, he's sitting with a girl*—

But what'm I supposed to do, I can't talk to anyone, I can't write it down, I can't show it to anybody, nobody knows it about me, to anybody else I'm just shy or quiet—

Or they see me for a fucking actor, false, afraid, they don't see why I act—

Alone—

What's the point of it then, if I can't use it, just tripping over all of it, what's the point of being able to talk, being able to think, dragging myself around in this stupid body that doesn't make any sense, what's the point if it's all clumsy and dishonest and scared and full of crap—

I want to look someone in the eye but I can't—

What're the point of eyes if that's the end of them, if I can't look at anybody, if I don't want them to look at me, what's the point of eyes, I want to look at someone and let them look at me, why don't I take my eyes out if I can't do something with them—

At least blind I wouldn't fuck with these fucking games—

But whatever the reason for my feelings, *they are my feelings*, and if they're just being blown out of proportion, I'm sorry, *they're serious to me*—

About the only thing that *is* serious to me.

* * *

And I used to want to tell my parents, *Listen, although suicide is as common in my mind as what to eat next, I have the common sense and will power to not do it, don't worry*—

But what's the point of that, if I can't even tell it to them—

And it's their fault I can't tell them—

How great it would've been to tell them that I think about suicide, and that I think about it all the time, but not like I'm going to do it, but just that I think about it—

How much it would mean to *just tell them that*, without mom going nuts, without dad taking the entire thing personally, saying how they've never done anything to make me feel this way, how it's just stupid of me to think that way and he'd refuse to imagine it, while mom can't help but imagine it and would just cry or worry, just tell dad to take the door off my room or take all of my belts, stupid shit, meanwhile I know where all the guns are and they're not going to hide those somewhere else—

I can't tell them, I can't explain it, I can't try to say that it has nothing to do with them, they never did anything wrong, dad would just say that doesn't make any sense—

And that's the point, it doesn't make any sense, that's why it hurts—

It doesn't mean it isn't real because it doesn't make any sense, it means it hurts more because it doesn't make any sense and won't leave me alone—

Why can't I just tell them, or somebody, it would mean so much if I could—

But I can't without it seeming like an alarm—

Just to tell someone would make it stop, I'm sure of it, but they'd never see that, and why not, why the hell not, why the fuck not—

Why is all of this so fucking hard—

I'm supposedly someone to care for, to think about, to give a shit about, but through nobody's fault I can't remember the last time I felt like anybody cared for or thought about or gave a shit about me at all—

I can't remember it, and if it happened, I couldn't see it—

But I can't tell anyone without them wrapping me up and taking me somewhere—

It's not that serious, but it is, *it is that serious*, but that's not the way to do anything about it, just take me somewhere and lock me in a room—

And it's even worse, my parents, they don't drink, they don't hit me, they don't yell at me, they've been married twenty years, and everyone else I talk to, they get hit, their parents are assholes, they drink, they swear at them or hit them, they say things like *I love you but I don't like you*, but I've got none of that and yet I feel this way.

* * *

It's so ridiculous I'm ashamed—

Church is fucked and stupid and I laugh when they say sin, but I know what shame is, I'm ashamed every fucking day—

The biggest and most impossible fantasy of mine is that I would kill myself, return the next day to school in someone else's body, and try as best I can to get an honest answer to the question *What did you really think of me?*, and after getting my answers, I would return to the day before, alive and well, knowing the true feelings of others—

That would fix me, if I just knew—

I can't ask, I see everything everyone does, and I analyze it, sometimes I'll stereotype them, I use my judgment to guess what they think of me, but never really truly know—

I become obsessed with the memory of a bad or a good look that probably wasn't directed at me, or a glance or a laugh or whatever, and I'll create others' opinions of me without their input at all, and then I like or dislike them because of all this, and all of this is based on looks that probably weren't even directed at me, it's all based on shit and based on nothing, how I spend my entire day just based on nothing, and I avoid or can be friendly to a certain few, because I think they like me—

They seem to anyway—

But in a way I'm not telling everything, I may just be acting again, *but I can't help that, this is as honest I guess as I can get—*

This is the best I can put it, it's so hard to find words for this—

It's isn't about shooting anybody, you tell somebody you want to kill yourself and they think what you mean is you want to shoot up the school—

People don't treat me bad, they just don't treat me at all—

I hate them, but not because they pick on me—

If I wanted to shoot anybody it'd be myself—

Those kids on the news, I understand them, but that's not what this's about—

Of course it's the kids with guns who get all the attention, I'm harmless except to myself, and as long as I'm the one in danger nobody cares, so I'm safe—

Fuck them—

Sure I get mad at girls, they ignore me, or only ones with boyfriends talk to me, but I don't want to kill them—

One girl I know, I wish I could talk to her, I heard somebody talking about her, her parents are divorced and her dad's remarried, but she lives with her mom and her little brother, I've heard her tell her friends about that, how hard it is, and I just want to talk to her, I hear her behind me and I just want to turn and talk to her, I want to say how I feel—

I imagine the two of us at the football games on Friday, walking around the track and ignoring the game, or just leaving the game early, going somewhere else entirely and talking, I watch my own steps on the sidewalk at night and I think what the sound of hers would be next to mine—

I wonder what it would be like to be funny with her, if I could, take her shoulders and tell a joke and make her laugh—

I never cried about a girl but I cry about her, when I think about her, if I could do that, if she could stand my voice and I could stand hers and we could talk and listen—

I look and see her and see pain and the same kind of alone in me—

I even see her with her friends, people talking, she's quiet sometimes and I watch her—

And I just know, I just know, if I could just talk to her, I just know we could help each other—

And not like a fucking doctor, not that help, because that doesn't help, like we're paying each other to talk to each other, not like some kind of chore, *you two are both sad, wouldn't it be nice if you both went and talked to each other*, but I mean really, I can't stop thinking about her sometimes, what it would be like to talk—

And I'm sure if that happened, when I feel like this I could think of her, and how we talked, and how this awful feeling won't last, I could think about her and be okay—

I see her in the hallway, she walks by and dresses weird, I want to say that even though I don't dress weird, we have things in common, we could talk—

But it'd be nothing, she'd listen to me for a minute at best, and she'd see how lucky I have it, and tell me off—

Alone—

I've got nothing to be sorry for, she's got assholes on all sides of her, the only asshole around me is me—

Or a girl in my geometry class, the bell's about the ring one day and I just turn my head and happen to see her and look past her, and she just says something like *That's real nice*, because I had some look on my face, I have no idea what it was—

How can I do anything, how can I, I don't know how I sound or how I look or what my face does—

Years ago at baseball practice, I was still little then, they had people try to bunt, and when it was my turn I couldn't do it, *I just couldn't do it*, I tried and tried and later some kid says it looked like I wasn't trying at all—

I never tried to do anything harder in my fucking life than I tried to bunt those fucking balls, and nobody saw it—

And even worse, they saw the exact opposite, how lazy—

Or in grade school I was biting my nails like I was at home, and I don't know why I did it, I bit one off and flicked it behind me, landed on some kid's desk, a friend, I see him out of the corner of my eye brush it away, stare at me, I'm too scared to say *I'm sorry* or *I don't know why I did that*, I just freeze and act like it didn't happen and look even more like an asshole—

This is all so complicated, my head explodes that this has been going for so long, I can't put it right.

* * *

So how am I supposed to approach a girl, or talk to a girl, or try to see if a girl likes me, or find out she does and ask her out, and go out with her and hold her hand in public, and talk to her on the phone, how'm I supposed to do any of this when my voice won't let me, my body, my face—

That seems impossible, how do you know somebody so well that you can see them naked and let them see you naked when you can't even stand to see yourself naked, my body is sick and I have no control over anything, I can't talk to anybody—

I don't even jerk off, I can't even do that, I've never tried, I just think of my dead grandparents or my neighbors watching and I can't do it, I can't do it that way and it all comes out while I'm sleeping and mom has to wash my underwear and it's all just shame and sick—

Don't tell me this is how I'm supposed to be—

I can't imagine showing myself to anybody, I hate how my underwear dries yellow after that happens, and I know everyone knows about it—

Or I wake up in the middle of the night to piss, I sit down to piss, dad's sleeping in the next room but I know he'd be awake if he heard me, I think if he heard me he'd be timing it somehow, he'd be assuming mine was big or small by how long I pissed—

How stupid, my dad with a fucking stopwatch at four in the fucking morning timing how long I'm fucking pissing, like that means anything, like that even sounds fucking reasonable—

But it's all I do—

It's all I fucking do—

It's all I fucking do and I cry about it and am scared to

death and I feel relieved but it just comes back—

It's all I do—

That and a million things like it, tear myself apart with it—

I fantasize about girls, I like a certain girl for a month or a few months, one of them I liked for almost the whole school year, some pathetic replacement for what I should be doing, I imagine whole conversations, things I do myself I imagine doing with her, how I would do it, a movie or whatever, I'd hold a door for her or buy her dinner—

Yeah, and with what money—

And when I stop liking her it's just like breaking up is in movies, it's ridiculous, I feel sad for awhile and then not, and when I see them again I feel sad but happy at the same time, some dumb shit feeling, it's like I've experienced something but I haven't, it's all just garbage, it's all just in my head, it means nothing—

I haven't said a word or done a thing except in my own head, my own head that betrays me—

All I've actually seen and done is seen her—whoever she is at the moment—walking down the hallway with somebody she wants to talk to, not even a guy she likes, just a guy, doesn't matter who, and how the guy makes her laugh and how she shoves him in that silly way girls shove guys who make them laugh, how they lift their heads when they laugh, how their cheeks rise and their eyes squint when they laugh, that's all I see—

That's all I fucking see—

I see that—

And I want to tear at them I'm so angry, and I sit in the car or I drive home and I shut the door, and there's nothing, it's all just shit—

Alone—

I can't say this at all, I can't even say it.

* * *

On the weekends I barely leave the house, sometimes I don't, in the summer it's even better, I count how many days it's been since I actually stepped outside, in grade school it was how many days since I washed my hands, or when the mailman comes I stand in the garage for a minute, five minutes, waiting and making sure no one else is walking or driving down the street, I don't want to see anyone walking or driving by, I don't want to say hi or say the wrong thing, I don't want to say nothing, I don't want their looks because of whatever I say—

I don't want to see anyone—

I just wish there was one person I could be alone with, one person I could ask to stay—

But there isn't, just a three-minute twenty-two-second song I listen to on repeat—

No singing or words, might as well not be listening to anything—

Tell me I shouldn't kill myself, just tell me and I will—

I tried to sleep two nights ago but my head was going all over, I rolled around in bed, turned on every side, opened the window—

I put my head on the sill and looked out at the street and it was so quiet, no cars going down the street and none going by on the main roads—

And I almost, I just almost, it was like I was there and then there was this wind and it was so quiet, and I heard the leaves falling from the trees onto the roof, against the window, it was so quiet and I thought I was calm, I was finally calm, when a car drives by—

And it took everything in me to not jump out the window and off the garage to chase that car, to just stand up and scream—

It's like a bug in the middle of my head that I can't dig out—

And the wind was blowing in and rattling my door and I was sure mom or dad had to hear it, they do every other night, and I waited by the door for them to get up and tell me to close my window, or put a shoe in the door, or just yell it from the next room, but it never happened—

Even they don't give a shit, I'm so confused—

Alone—

I don't want them to bother me, I'm sick of their nagging all the time—

But I want them to bother me, I want them to notice, I want them to hear the door rattle and know that the window is open and that I can't sleep, I want them to know everything I can't say, and tell me what I can do to fix it—

And I open my door and go downstairs and there's nothing, *nothing*, nothing and not a sound from their room, I'm sure they're ignoring me, I'm sure they don't care, they don't have anything to worry about, nothing keeps them up at night, they decide to go to sleep and it's over in a second—

And I go to the couch in the living room, and I kneel there, and it must be midnight, and the street is as quiet as it was upstairs, and the lamps outside light up the houses, the driveways, the garbage cans, the lights in other windows, it's all in black and white, it's not even a real world, those trees in the front yard I go by when I'm mowing the lawn, those aren't the same trees I saw then, they were pure black in the dark—

And I pound the only thing I can that keeps this quiet, I pound the cushions of the couch, and I remember that I'm kneeling in front of the couch in the same place as my father, in a picture of me after I was born, holding me in his lap—

And why the fuck did they make me, to feel like this—

I throw myself at the couch and I throw myself at the noise in my head, everybody's eyes and all their voices, and I keep looking at the steps, *I keep looking at the steps,*

I keep looking to the steps to see my mom come down the stairs to see what's wrong—

Don't they know there's something wrong, has there ever been anything more obvious in the entire fucking world—

Nothing—

Alone—

Not even a bad dream is waking them up—

I used to think something that would calm me, I used to think of a space ship blasting off from earth, and I'm just looking down as it goes, and I see everything get smaller until I'm out into space and even the biggest things get smaller, the earth, the other planets, the sun, I'm going away from all of them until it's just black and so dark I don't even know if I'm moving—

I don't even know if I'm moving—

I tried to think of that, I tried to think of that, I tried to think of floating and quiet, *I tried but my head wouldn't let me*, I just wanted to crack open my fucking head and pour it out and not think this way anymore—

And I know where all the guns are, I know where all the guns are because dad told me where they are, in case there was ever a burglar, over the mantle and atop this shelf and under his bed—

And I thought how I could get to that quiet I was imagining, I could get to it with just a run to the mantle and swallowing the thing, and I'm gone—

And I thought how I would never wake up ever again on a Monday, or on a Thursday I wished were a Friday, how I would never have to wake up or eat or walk ever again, no more eyes and no more listening and no more anyone—

No more wanting anyone and no more wishing they wanted to be with me—

Nothing—

But it's always my mother, I think of how it'd all be over in a second, it'd be so easy, but I know she'd be the one to find me, my mother I'm nothing but a trouble for—

I've thought of taking one of those guns and driving somewhere, anywhere, it doesn't matter, it could be on top of a mountain a million miles away, and they could report me missing, and the entire world could know I was missing and go looking for me, and I could shoot myself in a cave in India, and she would be the one to find me, the same as the kitchen downstairs, her only child with his head blown off and why did I do this, and she kneels and lays me across her lap and screams and sobs, and I can't do that to her—

I thought of telling them off, I think of what the most horrible thing I could say to them would be, to where they'd kick me out of the house and say they never want to see me again, but they'd never do that, I'd never say a horrible thing and they'd never react that way, neither of us are that way, even though for some reason I'm also *this* way—

I'm actually so lucky, and it's only the thought of her coming to my grave that keeps me from it—

And that's it really, that's how silly I am, some woman I can't talk to and who can't talk to me—

I'm willing to put up with sixteen or twenty hours of this shit a day, just on the off chance that someone whose house I live in might talk to me, or me to her—

But I'm sure it's me who ignores her, it's not her fault—

It's not her fault, it's not mine, I wouldn't know how to talk to me either, it's nobody's fault, it's just shit, this is just how it is, I can't even talk right—

Alone—

I act, and I'm nobody, and so's everybody else, how couldn't they be—

Everyone's stupid, everyone's afraid—

The people my age who act like they aren't afraid will just grow up to be like our teachers or my parents, acting and nobodying and doing nothing, fuck them.

* * *

Tell me where there's an adult that isn't just a kid, I used to think being older meant something, I remember I was five and dad said he'd play catch with me at night, but then he couldn't, something came up, it was the first time that happened—

It just shattered me being that little, and being lied to by my father—

Not actually lied to, but that's how it felt, I was only

five, what did I know—

And in grade school, after some kid gets beat up, and the pastor takes everybody in our class, all the boys, and we're in this tiny room for two days, two whole days of trying to see who did it and why, telling us how to treat other people, I had nothing to do with it but was put in there with them, and so many others, none of this is fair—

Everybody just tells me to figure out a way, to just get through high school, everybody goes through this when they're young—

They just tell me I'll grow up and get married and have a house and two cats and then a little baby—

Fuck that, that doesn't do anything for me now, tell me I'll have a wife and I'll see her one day sleeping on our couch and wake her up so we can go to bed together—

Fuck that, *when*—

Ten years from now, twenty, just five, I can't even see past next Monday—

Everything is so uncertain, I cry at music or a movie or a memory and feel I've gone away from this, but then come out of it and everything else is just how it was—

I won't make it till then, I won't make it till thirty, I can't stay here anymore—

The people who ignore me, they're mean and cruel and stupid, they don't know a thing, they can barely read or talk—

And the girls who ignore me, fuck them, they're whores, they wouldn't look good with me and that's all they think about so fuck them, I don't need them, all they do is live for people to fucking look at them—

I used to think being older meant something, but it means being exactly how you are now, except with more money—

I can't stand other people—

I don't want to think about them, I don't want them to think about me, I want to be left alone—

And somebody said this once in one of our classes, how fake and acting and insincere everything is, and the teacher comes back with God, *You can't leave God out of this, once you bring God in it all changes*—

Bullshit, God's a funny one, I used to pray every night, now I don't pray at all, I don't see any difference—

Because am I like this now because nobody's praying for me—

And do I deserve this—

I don't feel protected, I don't feel loved, I don't feel like there's any respect for anything, I don't think there should be, what does God have to do with it—

If God is how they say he is, God doesn't matter—

Dumbasses like to be shocking and say they don't believe in God, who cares, it doesn't matter—

All people want to do is be noticed, to shock—

I don't want to shock, I want to be left alone, I want quiet, I want my head to empty out and be quiet—

The only thing that calms me now is something else, it's almost too big for my head—

It's that there was never an earth, and never anybody on it, and then it's that there was never a universe, and nobody and no life, no stars or planets or heat, or those gasses, clouds, nothing moving *ever*—

And I keep going back and back, like in that spaceship, and all the lights go out, until I'm not even there—

And there was never anything, no life ever anywhere, nothing ever anywhere—

I see it in my head like a movie and it makes it hard to breathe and I smile, it makes perfect sense in my head, how big a thought it is—

Not if life never happened here, or if the past never happened just here, but anywhere, a simple huge nothing—

I imagine saying this to someone and I keep repeating it, *You don't understand, nothing ever, there was nothing ever anywhere ever, just a big whoosh*, and I make a vacuum sound at how empty it would be, how huge this emptiness, and I smile and they look at me weird because I keep repeating it but can never wrap my head around it—

I just can't say it right, but it's so great.

The Lake

WE'D PLANNED IT FOR YEAR. IT WAS AFTER WE SAW THE LAKE. WE TOOK a week off and got lost and ended up at the lake. We had time to talk, and time to think. We could stop. We sat by the lake and could sleep. Could wake. Could open our eyes and dream, with no before or after. A day of that, and we knew we were ready. That whiteness. The gold chains came in the mail today, *The welcome gift*, they'd said. We had nothing to sign. Only these chains, to be welcomed when we left.

The old place has been empty for more than a week. It's already our old place. Empty but for the bed, and what we're wearing today. We finished the food last night. We were happy we both decided to keep our boots here. It snowed like hell last night. We're buttoning our coats now, and can't do it fast enough. This is the last time we'll see the place. The last time we'll walk out the door and take the trash from the kitchen as we go.

Outside, the drifts are up to the windows of parked cars. The man across the street is stunning. He stands in the middle of the unplowed road in some huge black snowsuit. He is a dark stone in a bed of white. *Good luck*, he calls to us. He does not realize what he says. The TV suggests people stay home from work, and that is what he means. But we won't be coming back.

Our feet are already wet. The snow has nowhere to go but down our boots. Every annoyance is nostalgic already. No ploughs have come to any of our roads. Buses are stopped at angles further ahead. Pedestrians wander in the street like children on a playground. The cold is terrible, but no one is running. Today is slow, and that is enough. Cars are buried on either side of us. Humped in silence. Certainly along the sidewalk are many gifts—dog droppings, garbage, pumpkins from October, toys—that won't see the sun for weeks. That we won't see, ever. The white cat in the window we always pass is there too. White on white, she squints and grins on the sill. It is her world. We've taken off our gloves. Numb hands are warm hands. All things we do together.

The main road is barely one lane, from four. It's taken a half hour to get here. Cars are double-parked beside mounds of white, and from every direction snowblowers are heard from one block, two blocks, three away. We pass the building for the last time where I once saw its wall of ivy wave and sway in a spring wind. Rippling like water, flowing like the lake. Nearly there. Now that ivy is heavy and crusted. An old man slouched in his huge white coat.

We'll be free of all of this, in only a moment.

The subway steps are still too snowy to be slippery. Too few people have even tried to make it to the trains to melt enough of it away. So few of the usually hundreds of rushed or cautious feet. Down below, in the corner at the foot of the steps, like a man in white standing with his arms open, or a bird in beautiful wingspan, is a drift that came down the steps. It settled in the middle of the night, and spread. It whitens the drab station's black-greys and pale-yellows and dulled-silvers. Everyone who passes it smiles to see it there. So unexpected, a jewel in the drab.

Finally on the platform are actual puddles. Puddles left by those with melting coats and bags and boots. Melting hats and beards. Melting ring fingers. Those we recognize from our usual commute probably don't notice that we are without bags at all. If they searched our coats it might surprise them not to find a wallet. Not a phone. Not a pen. Not one used tissue, not even on me. If they noticed such things, they would find it strange that once on the train we aren't listening to music. That I'm not reading and underlining. That neither of us slept, as we went. These were all things we used to do. All past things. All things that would have made today's morning—slow, and with everyone soggy—easier to deal with. Music or sleep or words. All past. A sigh at what we used to do. We didn't even talk. At least aloud. Instead we touched foreheads. We ran our fingers up the others' arm, and smiled for the future. Or for the chink of the chain around our wrists.

We emerge from underground into daylight on the bridge overlooking the river and the city getting nearer. Everyone gasps, even we do. It has started up again, and no one has ever seen snow like this. The city, its buildings, have disappeared. The water below a nothing. Outside is only whiteness. The brief glimpses of the bridge seem the shadows of some dark shape far above us. Nothing is solid. Nothing is seen. The wind is furious but we can't hear it. The movement of the snow and the movement of the train but the silence of both gives stillness to everyone, and it's only now we see that the lights have gone out in the train. But it is still fully lit, with falling white—

And everyone jumps as a window blows open at the far end of the train, and the couple sitting there holler and dash to the other side. Its windows blow open too. We breathe, and down toward us the windows all blow open and let in the wind, and let out everyone's alarm, and as we clasp hands we realize it's happening much sooner than expected, and we know there will be no last day, and in a moment we are swept up and our arms burn and become white with feathers and our necks burn and extend and become white with feathers, and our mouths become hard and dark, our feet dark and webbed, and the chain links us as we assume ourselves out in the air, white as swans are, deep in the storm and white with it, the lake getting closer now.

A Ram in the Thicket

The ram Abraham sacrificed in place of Isaac
had been waiting for him there
from the sixth day of creation.

– Rabbinic Tradition

I AM NOT A GOOD PERSON. I WALK AWAY WHEN I SEE THEM COMING.

It isn't that they want to talk—it's that they talk so much, they have no one to talk to, and something about my face encourages them. So I don't let them see it, anymore. When I get far enough away and turn around, and act busy, they're pained, since they hoped to put their arms on the ledge and tell me something for ten minutes.

I can't take it, the questions and the things they laugh at, their desperation, their gossip about other homeless, who's on drugs and who washes their feet in the sink at the coffee place. They're in from the cold and come to a place filled with the employed, like me, serving people with lots of money—and they want to belong, they want that transaction life, they want to talk about the game from Sunday, they wonder where the guy from third shift went, I hate it. They shouldn't want my life.

I'm not a good person because I can't talk to them. I can't respond, I can't listen. I want to shut them up after five minutes. Once when the place was forced to close at night, ahead of a snow storm, I saw one of them two days later, a woman my age, wondering why we'd closed. When I said, "The snow storm," she scoffed, and when I added, annoyed, "So the people who work second shift could get home before it started," she wanted to spit, I could tell. Nobody gave that much of a shit about where she slept, she had nowhere to go, and with our doors unexpectedly locked during a blizzard, she had to go somewhere else, in the middle of the night. She didn't say any of this, but it was in her crooked mouth.

* * *

There's the drunk, with his can of beer, I never know if it's the same one, he swigs it too easily for anything to be in it. He comes in and looks at the tables and leaves, and does it again later, and finally comes back to start asking for something. He'll go up to an old man and ask for money, the old man's just sitting there reading his paper, or a little paperback, he's that kind of old man with his pants high up and hunched over in his seat, not used to talking anymore, his wife dead for years.

"Money? I don't have any money."

And the drunk will say, "Money? You're a millionaire!

A millionaire, you are!"

And the old man will cough and say, "A millionaire!" and start to get flustered, and won't know what to say, and he just gestures at his cup of coffee, or his coat, how none of that means a millionaire.

Then the drunk'll go up to a young guy with his headphones on, a quiet one, and rather than refuse him outright, he'll say something like (people like him always do), "I don't have any cash on me, sorry." Even if it's a lie, it's meant to not be rude. But the drunk will just say, "Come with me then. To the store. I'll go with you, to the ATM."

And when the kid realizes it hasn't worked, he'll just apologize again, and the drunk will stumble away to a third, another thirtyish guy with more attitude, and he'll just come out and tell the drunk to fuck off, mind your own business, get a job, screw you, and the drunk'll try to get him into a fight, but the tough guy will just wave his arm, wave his hand, "Fuck off," and go back to his food, not even look at him. And that has to be the worst, he won't even look at you.

Then the drunk will find a fourth, somebody who doesn't know English very well, and nervous enough as it is. He'll have his headphones on too, and whenever the drunk starts to ask, the guy will feign not hearing him, and point to his headphones, and put his head down, scared to make a scene. And I've seen it happen a few times—when the drunk finds one like this he'll sit down across from him and stare, and wait. I've seen him sit across from some guy for half an hour while the guy read his paper and kept his headphones on. It was terrifying.

If I was one of them I would be a fifth—I would never tell him to fuck off, I would never tell him I don't have any cash (I'm a horrible liar, and got rid of all my credit cards and lost the rest when my wife died), I wouldn't guffaw, amazed, at being called a millionaire—that only works for old men, and I'm not quite there yet. No, I saw him one morning and just gave him the first bill I found, to not look at him, to not have to talk.

* * *

The woman who scoffed about the snow, she was the one I didn't know was homeless for the longest time. When I first met her she said she knew famous writers, and that a really famous one who'd just died was really kind, though his wife was a burden; there was another writer she knew before he was famous, and she said, "Whenever I saw him he said he was still working on his book," and it turned out to be some classic, made into a movie that won all these awards. When I heard the first story I was happy, and told my coworker about it. "She's crazy," was all he said. When she told the second story, I didn't believe either one. It was sad. I thought she was telling me something good—this famous face, he was actually nice and human. Really she was just dropping names. My hair and my glasses, someway how I talk, have always made people think I read a lot, or even write, which is funny. She wanted me to know she knew the same people I supposedly did. She knew about movies and books. But I didn't know them. I knew the names. But I never read the books, I never even saw the movie. It looked boring.

I can't talk to them. I don't know why. I don't feel useless—how some people say, *I can't help them, there's so many of them*, and they make it a whole thing: *There's so much suffering in the world, I don't even want to see it, what good is it to help just one, there's so many.* That's bullshit. I remember when I was eight, and I was on vacation with my parents, I heard about a shooting somewhere, not even in our state, and two or three people died. My memory is odd, so long ago, but I can still remember how it felt to think this then, because I didn't understand why all these people were outside in lines with candles—sure a few people are dead, but there are still billions of people left! That's bullshit too, but I thought that when I was eight, but these adults are still doing it.

I can't talk to them because there's nothing to say. I feel ridiculous. I wake up and get to work as late as possible and leave as early as I can, and I watch crap on TV at night. I make just enough to get by, I can't do much. On the weekend I'll eat a little better, maybe find some woman, whatever, maybe not, probably not, I just end up talking about my wife. My friends are all assholes, I stopped visiting them, I couldn't talk to them anymore, I don't understand what they like, or what I used to like, I don't know anybody else. How does that compare to that woman's life? Begging for food or eating crap while I throw away whatever I don't use when I order too much, while I get a little fat, or I just forget I have it and have to throw it away when it smells and I remember?

Once I came in late, and the woman asked me why—they're around so much they get to know your schedule. I told her I had a dentist appointment, and then felt terrible saying that much. Because you can usually tell by their teeth. If you see somebody dragging a lot of bags behind them, and they look tired and a little sloppy, they could just be traveling. If their clothes look odd or dirty, they could have just woken up and be in a hurry, or just not care about dressing too well to come in here, and why would they? If they fall asleep in front of one of the computers—well, whatever, I guess that's a good sign too, and if they smell, fine, I don't know, that's the real telltale sign, some guy smelling like piss. But I can always tell from the teeth, brown and black and crooked, or just missing. Like she wants to hear about me going to the dentist, how does that make her feel?

But then, you know what, I was talking to her once and she told me the girl who worked on the other side of the store—the young one I make a dumb joke with every time she comes in, but never talk to—the woman said she made jewelry, had a jewelry design business on the side, said everything she wears she made herself. I've known the girl four years and I never knew that. And this homeless woman does, and is happy for her, she just said, "Everybody's got a business on the side today, you have to." But I don't, I've got shit, nothing. I'm the only person I know without a cellphone, or even a new coat. The drunk I gave money to has a better coat than me.

*   *   *

One of them is bald, a black guy maybe fifty or so. He talks about how he was homeless when the Olympics came somewhere, and how they gave all the homeless free bus tickets anywhere they wanted to go, to get them out of sight. "That's not how I got here, though," he says, like he'd never choose to come here, and I want to ask him what's wrong with here. Instead I let him into the bathroom. He always calls me *young man* even though I'm probably older than him. He's got a huge rolling suitcase that I don't know how he pulls it all day long, and every time he leaves the store I envy him. I've just been told I'm working Sunday through Thursday now, this after I was promised no more weekends, this after I went from ten hours four days a week to eight hours five days a week, this after I nearly quit after the fourth manager was hired, all of them useless, all of them young and sure what they're doing is meaningful, and this after I thought I was done with these jobs when I was twenty.

One of the managers even slipped up once. People were

calling off all the time, and why wouldn't they, and he said at a meeting, and he stopped himself right away, "I know, we all know, we all have family emergencies, family things, but at some point you have to make a choice between work and family—" Some thirty-four-year-old with a wife and kids who prefers this garbage to his family, how about that? If he only knew. But apparently whatever he has with his wife is nothing. If he knew what I had he wouldn't even be here. I hope his wife dies, I do, I hope he has to bury her, and see what priority he gives this shithole.

I almost want to be one of them. The one lady who sits at the table hours on end with her tiny Bible and a magnifying glass, everything she owns on the table or around it, a huge hood tied with a kerchief over her head that covers her face, so that I don't even know she's a woman, only that she's fat and bundled up even in the summer with her magnifying glass and her Bible. Or a huge leather-bound thing, one volume of the dictionary, a law book, whatever, it doesn't matter. Why can't I be like that, why can't I sit in my own dirt and hang my head over a table all day and stare at nothing, read words that mean nothing?

Or another guy, been carrying around the same book for years, has he read it, read it ten times, again? What book is worth reading that many times? Or another, talking on a cellphone he doesn't have, talking to somebody who isn't there, talking about what another person who isn't there is eating, over and over? Or another, like an act, it's hard to believe he's crazy since he's so predictable, it's seems so planned, he'll stand in front of the pop machine and stare, and lean forward, and lean back, and stare, and stand, won't move, and then leave for a half hour or hour or five minutes later, and come back, the same, and leave, all day— what bliss that must be, to forget. Instead I have to come behind this counter everyday for some responsibility, for some memory I'm killed by, for some life I promised, *Go on without me.* You would agree to anything somebody says, dying in a bed and begging you to go on, I'm not saying I didn't mean it, but you would say anything. I had no idea what I was saying. *Live without your lungs*, she might as well have said.

I want to go to the woods and hunt, build a fire and eat what I've caught. I did that a long time ago. I want to enter the day like I used to enter the woods, I knew what I was supposed to do but didn't know how it would happen. There's no chance of that now. There's just the same parking-lots and streets and stop-lights, and then the reverse at night. Nothing unexpected is even possible, nothing better, nothing worse, just mournful.

Back then I turned to my wife, or I called my father on Friday for a moment, he would put my mother on toward the end—now sealed lips, my wife gone and grey, and all of them gone, and I've no children because I said I would make no father. But how it would be now, to see her face still here in my home, in some growing body, some child of ours, a teenager even.

*   *   *

The woman with the teeth knows everybody, even if it's just gossip. They all know her name. And the ones who meet in the morning all come from the same shelter, the same boxes, the same corner, they shower in the same places that let them, they stop and talk and chatter. Even the crazy ones who talk to nothing become lucid in a moment and shake the hands of the faces they know. They are all a family, they all know what to say. The church across the street lets them put their boxes up at night, it's horrible but uplifting to see, they do it together, they bring their boxes. In the wintertime you don't know if the shapes up against the side of the church are snowdrifts or people, snowdrifts or their boxes.

Then the other day there was a terrible sound from the back, we all ran and came to the bathroom, and a man was on the floor beside an overturned trashcan, his pants were draped over the towel dispenser and wet towels and his own shit were all on the floor. It didn't matter what had happened. He was old as my father when he died, white hair and skinny-old the way elderly are, frail and pathetic, you could snap him, but a baby again, overwhelmed but shamed but enjoying it somehow, there was a light in his eyes. And when all anybody else could do was stare or cover their mouths I stepped in to pull him up, and both our hands muddy he took mine and another on my shoulder and said, "The oak tree where they sit, the oak tree no one sees, the oak tree that is garbage."

They let me go home after that, since I didn't have an extra uniform pants or shirt, and the young manager acted like he'd never smelled shit before. They said take tomorrow off too. I only heard somebody being sent home early, I only heard of that happening once, when a new hire was spit on by a customer, and nearly jumped the counter. Whatever they saw, they didn't see me lunge in to help him up—they could only believe that I'd been forced to the ground, slipped, they couldn't believe I'd gone in there to help. And they hadn't heard what he said. So I cleaned up, and somebody found some jeans and a shirt in the basement and there I was, leaving at three in the afternoon on a weekday, it was incredible. I wanted to drive around with my wife like we used to, we'd go anywhere, she'd say *Take a left* or *Take a right*, or we'd see a building or a water tower far away and try to drive to it, for hours, she'd have her favorite music on shuffle, she'd tell me all she was going to cook. Being in the car alone is worse than being at home that way, I get lost so easy and there's no joy in it.

* * *

I spent the evening doing nothing, no lights or TV, no food. The lights were usually to keep me up so I got something to eat, the TV to keep me busy while I ate, the TV so there wasn't silence before I went to bed. I did take a shower, but not to prepare for the next day at work. I sat in a chair in the dark and recollected, something I hadn't done in a long time. Usually memories would take me over when I was doing something else, when I couldn't focus on them, and got annoyed. Now there were only memories, in the chair in the dark in the quiet.

Long after evening, a light came into my face. I never slept in the living room, so never knew about this light. It came from behind the building, and flickered. I went to draw the shade and when I saw the scene—a lamppost, a dumpster, an oak tree—I remembered what the guy said. I'd never gone back there either, it was where the old parking lot had been, and only the super took our trash out to that dumpster. But now I went out there with a shovel and started digging. I hid behind the dumpster whenever I heard anything, a shade go up, you can hear a head peek out and gaze with judgment.

It took awhile, but I heard something. It should have been shovel hitting metal that I heard, but instead it was the sound of her, a laugh or a breath, I heard her gasp. I bent down and loved to dip my hand in that dark, and amid the dirt I felt cool steel, ridges, something embossed, beaten out. A few more minutes and I had a bowl, a big cup, impossible, it was beautiful, what had it been doing there? It was filled with faces and things that spoke to me as I turned it in my hands. I forgot where I was and just sat beside the dumpster under the light and spun it and stared: there was a bearded man, and nearby was a small boy, and they held their hands up to pig. There was a dog, and a horse with wings on the shoulder of a man. A man leaps over a bull. A man holds a deer by his horns. A woman holds a bird in one hand and a man in the other, while above her a girl plaits her hair. A man fights a lion, a man boxes. A man holds a dragon, holds a snake. There was a man between many animals, and he had horns on his own head, and his legs were crossed. There was a wheel and a broken wheel, a woman's head and a man's head surrounded by wheels, an elephant, a dragon, a dog. There is a horned snake, another man with horns, a helmet with horns, a lion with wings. There are three huge animals dying under the swords of three huge men. There is a line of men in arms, and at the head a large man is being dipped into a bowl.

I am invigorated.

And the bowl smelled of her. I can't say how. I looked around as if someone were to take it from me, as if someone saw me. But there was no sound, only the smell of all her cooking, coming from the empty bowl filled with dirt. And it seemed to me that it had been waiting for me there since before I was born.

As I walked back to the building, I saw a man much like me, and he dug in the cold with ungloved hands through the garbage, and he grabbed at cans and bottles for the shopping cart he dragged alongside him. The sound of those cans was the first sound I heard since I threw the shovel to the ground, and when the man saw me, and saw that I stared, he shook and took a step back. He smelled, he needed, he crouched and folded. But I stepped forward and gave him my hand, and I felt my mouth open and I heard words come out. And when he came with me through my front door, there was her warm bread on the table.

Unburdened

THERE'S NOTHING WRONG WITH BEING A MOTHER, I'M NOT BEING CHEATED out of anything, I'm not missing anything, I'm no less than my husband who works. (But I am glad it's him who goes everyday, I've never been able to do that, I can't stand people, it's enough to walk past them here in the parking lot.)

All this rubbish, from the teenagers who don't want to become like me, to the fifty-year-olds who wish they'd never been me who stick their asses out and wear what a teenager wears all over again—and who knows how much plastic surgery. Who's paying for that? I don't use money for myself like that, I would feel so guilty, those women who spend all their husband's money on clothes and jewelry, I hate jewelry. Or planning those awful beach vacations and starving yourself until you get there so some slob can drool over you, or so some other woman can feel jealous.

And don't give me all that college crap, I would've been there burning my bra, I'm not an idiot the way they look at me, it doesn't seem too freeing to pretend you're young forever, pretend you don't want babies, or that if you have them you treat them like your dogs, or some new outfit you want to show off. It's not babies or jobs but what women have to put up with, and what we do to put up with it, and how we make it worse, we never make things easier.

And I hate the grocery store the most. If I could come in the middle of the night I would, I only come here twice a month, once for the real food, the second time for the junk stuff, it's always the looks I get when I come for the junk stuff, they see the pop hanging off the sides, the potato chips, the microwave dinners. They look at me like I'm five-hundred pounds even though I'm hardly bigger than I was in college, I don't need to diet again and again like them, I'm basically happy. They got organic everything in their carts, they come in here with their yoga mats and their cellphones, they don't look up from them unless it's to look down on me, they're no better than me, I don't need to walk around like that to feel good about myself, I don't care what anybody thinks, they can go to hell.

Just because I have to tell the little one to get back here constantly, she's only four, I never had a grocery store like this when I was that small, I'd be doing the same thing! They look over at my hand to make sure I've at least got a ring on—I'm no single mother. But nothing pleases them, because if I *were* a single mother then it's that horrible word, it's *empowering* somehow, it means I don't need a man, but if they see I have two kids and aren't married, they judge you anyway. If they see you are married, now that's the worst, they check your feet to make sure you're not barefoot—they check your belly to make sure you're not pregnant, again.

But the women my age aren't any better, they're actually worse, have you ever met a worse human being than a woman with a ten-year-old boy or girl who's realized all of a sudden she never should've had children, and who does all she can with every hint to mention how she wanted to go to college, how she wanted to travel, how she wanted to do so many things, but her asshole of an ex-husband kept her from it, and then left her and the kids, and aren't men just pigs?

Those're the worst, they stand there all day with their daughters selling those cookies right in front of the store, making your daughters pathetic, that's how they learn to grow up begging for money, it starts when they're ten when they sit in front of the supermarket yelling at strangers to buy their cookies—that must be where it starts, where a girl finds out her voice sounds sweet to everyone. And the mothers hate it, they have to stand nearby all day long but make it look like their little princesses are selling these cookies on their own, they hate it and you can tell, but they herd together with the other mothers and stand together and act like they don't hate it, and the only way they can act like they don't hate it is if they make it seem like they love it, and that anybody not doing it is missing out. I'm so sick of being forced to envy somebody, or that somebody envy me.

And my little one sees the little girls and asks when she'll be old enough to do that, and I say never, she's *never* doing that, I won't ever see her act that way, it's not many steps from there to a bar in ten years, dogging yourself up for some idiot who probably can't spell your name even but he's handsome and you're young and you need it, that hard warmth in your hand, and it's all astoundingly good as long as you don't open your eyes, some man saying you're so beautiful to and you're the reasonable one who's in control and going slow and driving him crazy until you can, if you're lucky, finally just reach back and go completely crazy yourself, and lose yourself, and let go for once in your life, and feel like you aren't anybody anymore, you aren't somebody in high heels or tennis shoes or a godawful pantsuit or some work suit or even a wedding dress, just some great body containing that hard great warmth that leaves that warmth and that sting inside you, you feel like you're some great thing, something warm and real and honest, you feel that's what you were made to do, what people were made to do, if they could only feel that with the right person, what a great desperation sex is, like you're falling and falling and don't want to lose it, but you have lost it and that's why it's a thrill.

That is empowering, that and not talking about it afterwards with whoever'll listen, *that is* empowering, walking around with a grin for the rest of your life, knowing you know what's possible between people. I don't grudge anyone kissing and telling, but it's never true, it's just silly when you try to talk about it, it's all about control for them, they can talk about it like they were in control, like they were even two people at all, when it's really just losing control, and that's what we all want, women and men, and we're so dumb and stupid because of it.

* * *

I don't know what it is about us, it's not that we're getting older, we're only in our thirties, we don't talk any less, but our silences are different. Something isn't working. He's very sweet, he's so sweet, he remembers everything. But the way we talk anymore—our jokes are just about the past. We aren't growing, we just say *Do you remember when we did that?*

This sounds so ridiculous! How can you not grow when you have children! This doesn't have anything to do with sex. I can feel that closeness walking down the street with him. When you're so close to someone you get it from holding their hand, that can be just as warm. Or how he looks at me like he did when we first met. But that doesn't happen anymore. We aren't intimate. Sometimes we have sex and sometimes we don't, but it's always been that way. The problem is how I talk to him, and how he talks to me. The problem is how he looks at me, and how I look at him. He's not even crude anymore, I would kid him about being a man, obsessed with my boobs, he doesn't even do that anymore, he doesn't even do that so I can pretend I'm annoyed, sometimes I really was annoyed (they're just boobs for God's sake), but it was fun, it was attention, I know he loves me.

It's small things, there's no end to them, I never thought about them before, but they feel like a waste. I'm annoyed by the dishes now, I clean them and they get dirty and I clean them again. And clothes—washed, ironed, worn, washed, patched, repaired, washed, sewn, replaced. I hate it, I hate that it annoys me somehow, but it does. Or I come here every Friday, spend money on food, eat it, spend more money on food. I'm annoyed even having to go to the bathroom, that never happened before, even that feels now like the food I eat is a waste, what does it matter, I'm just going to end up flushing it down the toilet. I didn't mind any of this before. I liked making clothes last, I liked planning different food for the next week and stocking up the freezer, but then I was sick one week, I didn't do hardly any of that, and things just went on, there wasn't any difference, nothing I was doing was making any difference, it didn't matter if I did them or not. It's all irrational, I know I'm doing so much, I'm raising my children. But I feel anybody could raise them, anyone could push them in a cart, anyone could buy them food and cook it, there's nothing much special about me, about what I do.

* * *

I don't judge other women, I'm not catty like they are,

I'm not looking for complements. But something is wrong, I feel empty about everything. And I had a horrible thought the other month, I thought what it would be if they all died in a fire, if I got out and he ran back in to get them, and died too, died a hero and everyone sad and honoring them, and me getting all this attention, and if I got married again I could say I couldn't bear to have children again, with what happened to my first two.

I thought of all of my own things burned and gone, I felt nervous and excited, I was so ashamed. And then it happened—some family, I forget where, they had two sons, they died in a fire and only the wife got out, and the wife was left all alone. It was too close to what I'd thought, I saw it on the news and almost screamed, it felt like I was being spoken to, and they interviewed the wife and I had to turn it off, I saw her face and she looked empty and lost and I had to turn it off, I didn't watch it, I couldn't believe I'd thought that.

You see, I'm not like other women. I know women who would laugh at that mother, or they'd say something horrible about *That's what happens with love*, or with a husband, or with children, and that's why you shouldn't give yourself to anyone, you shouldn't care or feel anything because you never know when something horrible will happen. I'm not like that. I don't know of anything better than love, or giving myself to somebody, or feeling emotion. Or I used to. I don't feel I'm alive. Something has been flushed out of me, and I can't figure out what it is.

I'm not depressed, I'm not like those gloomy people who sit around all day sad, I couldn't stand that, they should just get up and walk around, maybe that would help, why would you want to be that way and just sit around? I'm not like that, I want to do something about it, and I'm sure part of this is because I have no woman friends. Well, I have no male friends either, but I think it's important for a woman to have friends who are women. But my only options are other mothers, neighbors on the street or parents of other kids at the school. I get along with a few of them, but the rest I can't stand, they know I don't like them and that I don't belong, and all they talk about is how little they eat, how much they've eaten, how they can't stop eating, how much they love food. I'm not in great shape but I don't care what they think of me. I only feel terrible about myself when I'm around them, why should I be friends with them?

Anywhere outside the house I'm walking on tiptoes, I go out of myself and watch myself and listen to myself the way I never do when I'm all alone, it's not healthy. There's no time I can come to the grocery store without there being a crowd of mothers who don't work during the day, or at night all the rest of them, who strut around proud because they work *and* they're mothers, and they can tell I don't work, I hate how they look at me.

* * *

The only woman I can talk to is from the church, I don't buy any of that anymore but we do go sometimes. She's the minister's wife and has a ton of kids, and we've always gotten along. But she doesn't live nearby and always seems taken up with church things, but I was able to go there one day when the kids were with my mother, and we sat in the cafeteria of the school there and talked for ages, it got to where I just cried.

I told her I was upset and didn't feel good as a mother, but I'm not one of those mothers who resents her children. I told her I was upset and didn't feel good as a wife, a partner, but that I'm not one of those wives who hates or resents her husband, who wants to cheat on him or thinks he's cheating on me. I told her I was upset at being at home all the time, but that I wasn't one of those women who wishes too late she did a bunch of things, I said over and over I went to college and did all that.

I couldn't believe I was telling her all of this, we know each other but not that well, and I couldn't believe she was sitting there listening to all of it, I could never do that, I can't listen to whining. She looked at me so kind, she said all of *Those women* I keep talking about, she said they don't exist, she said there are only people with problems, and when I started to talk she stopped me and told me she understood how some women really were bad mothers, or bad wives, or were just superficial, but that what they needed wasn't my judgment, and that I don't need theirs either. She said it was possible to wish you had done more before you got married, and not fall into some category of bitter women who're all the same. She said it was possible to feel abandoned by your husband and not fall into some category of some pathetic housewife. She said what I was feeling was important, and I shouldn't mix it up with something else, but that pissed me off, because I need to know, within myself, that I'm not like what all those other women are like.

But she didn't understand, she's all enclosed in her church and isn't in the real world at all, she just doesn't know what it's like. Her husband works all day at the church that isn't a hundred steps from their house, she doesn't have to worry about him being away all the time, coming home late, not knowing where he is, and their kids always have both of them around, just about. She's got it real nice, she can be like a housewife but she still does a ton of things with the church, church groups, all of that, so she looks at me like those women who have careers do, their heads in the air, I'm so sick of hearing that they "can have it all"—they don't have anything, they don't have anything at all, if they have to drop their kids off at daycare every morning, or even at a relative's, a mother and a father should be with their children, there's just no two ways about it, and that's why I am the way I am, and I won't be any different.

It's none of their business about my marriage, all they do together is talk about their marriages or old boyfriends.

I won't talk about any of that. I won't tell them anything. I'm not some kind of puzzle that you figure out, nobody is. What does it mean that I lost my virginity in college, after a dance, sitting up on a bathroom sink? That's not very romantic now is it? But just because it was awful doesn't mean it was some key to my fucking existence.

Because then there're the ugly girls, or just not the ones every guy jumps at, the fat girls, I was one of those until I went away to college, and all of a sudden I had all this attention and didn't know what to do with it, you just jump at it like it'll never happen again. I didn't want that slob on the bathroom sink to be special, I was just scared he wouldn't talk to me, or would tell everybody about me, I was half drunk anyway, I just had to get it over with so I could move on. How could it possibly be special with somebody like that, and why should it? Not everything is special, not everything means something, not everything should. It took a long, long time for it to become special, for it to mean anything at all besides the most selfish comfort, because it is comforting, to feel someone next to you, even if it could be anybody, I'll take somebody rather than nobody, and then wait for somebody special to come along. That's what I had to do, it made it so I wasn't desperate when I did meet my husband, I had a clear head and could see how good we were together, and that wouldn't've been possible if he'd been the first man I ever dated or slept with, I would've been nervous the whole time.

There were a lot of mistakes that got me there, but I don't know how else it could have happened, a lot of pain and stupidity, even what some people did when I was a little girl, making me sit on his lap all the time, touching me when I had a bathing suit on out of the pool, I knew it was weird then and it confused me for the longest time and I knew it wasn't right but a kid's powerless—even that was for my husband. If I'd killed somebody, that would've been for my husband too. If I'd been a spot different in any way, I don't know if I would've ever met him, if there would've even been that right mix of both of us being a little drunk, and so me being a little more assertive than him all of a sudden (that's how he gets when he drinks, he clams up and gets weak). If our past hadn't all happened just how it did, we would've never gone home, never even met, maybe—he would've had different friends, I would've been with friends that night and not been out alone, there's so much that goes into it. Which is why what's happened is so awful, I think it was all fated and meant to be, I don't feel like any of this was ever my choice, I feel so out of control with this—

And finally! I've been looking for him since I got in here, I don't know how many times I've circled all the aisles. He's some kind of supervisor, not a manager, but somebody high up, I've seen him a few times, the last time he helped me find something, he went into the back to get it. When he came back, when he came close and put something on a shelf, I could smell his face, I got some warmth from him, his eyes flashed at me. His hand touched mine and he laughed with me for a moment.

Now I would never do anything with him, but it's a thrill to be around him, to come here and find him, to see him for a second, to think about him sometimes and plan to be here, I've been thinking of him since last night, it kept me up. There was also a man at the library, another one at the gas station for awhile, and it used to be the mailman before they put someone else on our street. It's all teasing, I dream about some of them, in real life the most I ever touch are their arms but the dreams are just crazy, they're all married or they see I am, and it's some forbidden thing, it feels like playing with fire. If they ever tried anything I'd stop it right away, they couldn't ever claim I was coming on to them, I'm very careful, but we all know what we're doing, it's flattering as you get older to still be admired, even though nothing will ever come of it, and it's something you need because everything else is so lonely.

I push the cart towards him and he doesn't smile when he sees me but he nods, and something in his eyes, he does recognize me. He looks like he didn't wash his hair this morning, or maybe he showers at night before going to bed, I suddenly want to know all about him, take care of him, he's sweating a bit. He's helping the young kids stock the shelves, I bet he's a wonderful father.

We're talking and he moves closer to me, he moves around and looks down the aisle, he smiles at my daughter and at my son. He's so sweet. It isn't anything we're saying but just that we're talking, or that I feel people are watching us, that they think it's inappropriate somehow and will talk about it, think about it, look at me differently, wish they were me. The women older than me, they pass by and know this isn't my husband, and they understand, they have one of these men somewhere else, someone they talk to in public to get looks for, to feel recharged by, it reminds me of how my husband and I first met, and I love to feel something like that, I love him even more after, and I don't mean sex, that becomes so rote sometimes, I mean a real deep burning inside. I understand when I hear how prostitutes won't kiss the men but they'll still have sex with them, sex isn't intimate after awhile, it's like machines, intimacy and emotions are something else, I haven't felt an emotion during sex in years.

He breaking down a box and mentions some celebrity wedding that broke up, I think I know who he means and I laugh and say they deserve it, they weren't in love. But he laughs and says love is like Bigfoot. I don't say anything and he says, "Someone thinks they took a photo of it, but you'll never see it and you can't prove it exists." I back away from him and want to throw up, I want to get out of this, I take my phone out of my purse and start to say that someone's calling when there's screaming from the front of the store. He looks at me and apologizes and goes off, and I push my cart and get in line where I can see where the noise is. It's some mother and her little boy by the magazine aisle, he's screaming something but he doesn't sound right, it sounds like he's retarded. But she doesn't look upset, this must happen all the time, she's embarrassed. She catches my eye as she leads him out of the store and looks at my daughter—and she gives us a look, and I want to ask her who's she's looking at, it's not my fault she doesn't have control of her kid, but down another aisle I see him there again, talking to someone else, one of the younger ones with the yoga garbage, or they come straight from the gym still sweating and that's an excuse to wear what they wear in a grocery store, and she's standing with him too, right where I was. And he reaches up and gets something for her, they laugh together, and she takes his arm. Am I that blatant, I can't be, none of these people have anything to do with me—

I feel something terrible welling up in me like I'm going to be sick, I pull out of the line and go to the self-checkout and do it as quickly as I can, and somebody comes to help me bag and swipe my card, I don't even see any faces, I just pay and I leave, and I hate myself for driving to this store that's further from the house just to see him, I'm so ashamed and want to pull into a gas station somewhere but I speed home and I pull into our driveway and unlock the doors but I can't get out, and I tell the kids to go inside and I'll be right there, and when they're gone I start to cry. I refuse to believe that I'm like that.

* * *

I don't know what I have, I can't think straight, I'm in my car sobbing but I see the garage and how it needs to be painted, and how the couple next door needs new siding, and there're holes in their screens from their cats scratching, I can't even concentrate on crying, on why I'm crying!

The only time we nearly broke up, we were still in college and I had my own room and the air conditioning was out and it was so hot in my room, and most of our clothes were off because it was so warm, but we didn't have any money to get a big fan, and no room for it even if we had the money, but we were acting like we were breaking up and I was on the bed and he was on the floor away from me. He kept reaching up to touch my leg and I would bat him away, we were so sweaty and gross and I can't stand to be sweaty next to somebody whose sweaty too, neither of us could sleep, but we wouldn't talk, and it was so hot, and he finally put his hand on my thigh and I was half-awake but we were breaking up and so I kicked him, I kicked his hand away, and he swore at me, the first time he really did that in anger at me—he still didn't like to fight back then, that took years—and he started to put his clothes on and put his books in his bag and I could hear him tying his shoes and I started begging him not to go, and he didn't know what to say, he was still real quiet then and didn't want to say something awful, but that's how it was then, he'd be quiet so long and when he finally said something it would just be terrible and blunt, he said I was treating him like shit and that we were both ridiculous and he was leaving, and I just cried to him from the bed, *I don't want to be alone!* And he stopped and we both cried and he came back to me and we made love again and we were married a year later and that's all. Should I have let him go? Should it have ended there? Do I not even know—

The woman from the church is there, she's knocking at the window, I wipe my eyes and smile at her. She has a pan of brownies in her hands and I step out and ask her what's she's doing. She asks if I'm okay, and helps take the groceries in, and we sit down in the kitchen, and I make some coffee. She says I may have misunderstood her a few days ago, she wanted to see how I was doing. She even takes my hand! I can concentrate on her, taking my hand. And she asks if she can tell me a story. I tell her I'm not into all of that and she says it's fine, I don't have to be, she says it's about two monks but I could just make it about two anybody. And she tells me about two monks a long time ago, and one of them is young and feels guilty about the things he's done, and other is an older man and he sees the younger one needs help, and the younger one tells him it's his burden and he can't do anything about it, and the older one says he can whisper it in his ear, just whisper it to him, and give the burden to him to carry instead, he's old and he's used to it, and better at it, and he says when he whispers everything that's bothering him, he can forget about it, because it's not on his shoulders anymore.

And she looks at me, she's still holding my hand. She

says she knows it isn't even that easy, not that easy by far, that that's just a story, that even though it will take time to forget or move on I can still tell her, and that she has a strong back, heavy shoulders. And she laughs—she is a little short and fat, and she laughs at how she is, her wide shoulders. I want to laugh at how I am! So I try—I laugh too. And I close my eyes to concentrate. And we both wear wedding rings, and they tap together like some beat, and I search to find what I mean to say, it's so hard, I've never had to say what I mean before.

One Time People

A YEAR BEFORE I'D THOUGHT SO MUCH. PEOPLE IN DEBT WEREN'T ME ANYMORE. People with marriage problems weren't me anymore. People obsessed by whatever people get into, hobbies or careers or religion or politics or whatever, they weren't me anymore, I'd done all that and it was never quite real. Now I'm all of it, all over again.

We weren't rich, but we'd hardly any debt; we'd been together fifteen years, and still people stopped us on vacation to ask if we were on our honeymoon. I enjoyed a good book, a good documentary, I read about stuff I liked on the side, I'd a good job and went to church sometimes, but none of that swept me, they didn't matter so much that I became an asshole.

It'd taken years to achieve this, a calm balance between everything, we'd cleared so much away as a couple, I'd cleared so much away from my mind, I was happy, not enlightenment happy, not lottery happy, not the kind of happy you put on the news, but real happy, so much so we'd even thought about adopting children.

*　*　*

It was a Saturday and I was cutting the grass for the first time that year, it was up past my ankles and as I turned to make a pass a rabbit shot out from the standing grass and bounded down to where I'd already finished, by the railroad ties and the broken fence I'd always wanted to replace with a stone wall, ever since we vacationed in England and saw how the countryside, even the mountains, and incredibly like some magic trick, was covered in old stone walls criss-crossing everywhere.

Of course I'd never actually've run the rabbit over, but still the flash of doing just that came to me: its cry (would it cry out?), the spray of blood and insides, the red grass and the mangle I'd find when I turned the mower over to clean the blades—this's what I thought of.

*　*　*

There was an older woman I used to see on my lunches at work, all the time. I always thought she was eyeing me, but I doubt she ever was. She was tall, and taller in the stiletto heels she'd spent decades perfecting how to wear and walk in, I don't know how you do that, she never wore the same thing twice, but I remember once a red leather jacket and a tight skirt. She was maybe sixty with white hair, long, and she cinched it up in back right up against her skull so it spilled in a white line down between her shoulders. She walked straight-backed, clicking with great purpose whenever she came to where we ate lunch with a ton of others. She always had black sunglasses on, no matter the season. She was so tall, so apparently elegant, or just pretending—I don't know the difference—that I doubt if she dropped something she'd deign to bend over and pick it up, she'd just leave it there, bright red lipstick, horrid old white face, and red in the cheeks. She seemed so together, so confident, or just fashionable—I don't know the difference!—so sure of herself, but she was always alone, it was creepy to think she was looking at me, but then I felt sorry for her. She always had a paperback to read, if she had a phone I never saw her use it. She walked in like grace, obviously looked and acted differently than everyone else, left like grace, but didn't seem any happier than the people she was apparently different from, who were more sloppy, like me, so all that style didn't do her any good, it seemed like.

* * *

And just after the rabbit flew away I continued with the grass, keeping an eye out for others. I remembered as a kid this one time I'd seen a frog leaping out of the way of the mower, I'd stopped and picked it up, first to get it out of the way, but then, because we had no pets, we were always allergic, and since I was just little and liked these things, I put it on a shelf in the garage under a cup, since I wanted to play around with it later, and even having it in my palm as I carried it was something, its legs wrapped around two of my fingers.

But then I forgot it was there, and didn't remember for a week, and no horror movie was as scary as approaching that turned-over cup in the garage, and the garage was now really dark and dank and spooky, dusty, and I lifted the cup and it was just sitting there like a rock—and I stepped back because I thought it was still alive and was just staring at me, but then I nudged it with the cup and it was hard and soft, hard so that it didn't move like it was rigid, but soft like it was starting to rot, and when I found the courage to just sweep it over the edge into a trashcan I was holding up as I tried not to watch, it left a spot of slime on the old shelf.

*   *   *

After that Saturday I started to go the bar all the time, and the first time I didn't realize it was a college bar but I got used to it, it meant no one was going to talk to me— women, I mean, or they were really just still girls. They would squeeze in getting their drinks and giggle, but I had nothing to make them laugh, no line, no personality, no game, I didn't want anything to do with them, didn't even try. And the men they were after were their perfect match, so I wasn't a threat to them at all, I didn't dress or smell or sound like them even though I could've run circles around them talking sports statistics, stolen bases and batting averages and slugging percentages from the eighties, and a few of those guys I could've been friends with but I was closer to their dads' ages than their own, and you only have one father.

Except one guy, he was older than them but still younger than me, there was still a bit of rope connecting his age with mine, it wasn't a huge gulf. He was just as miserable as me, and when it got down to it he just told me that he'd been born and immediately given up, he'd grown up in an orphanage and never got adopted and had a horrid time going through school and all that, and said he'd found out—I don't know how, I don't know why he'd lie—he said his mother'd been college-age and he'd just been the product of a one night thing, didn't matter.

And when he finally came around to telling me all this, I had to piece it all together, I asked him if being at this bar of all places wasn't torture to him and I said there were sports bars and old dives and shitty corners where college kids wouldn't ever go so why does he come here where an unwanted kid just like him has a pretty good chance of being produced? And I said that'd be like me trying to forget about my wife by hanging out at the stadium where I'd dropped her off that morning for graduation but he said no, he said no even after showing me all the marks on his arms and all the attempts and all the drugs, he said no, they should be allowed their fun, he said there's not much either way and they're as lonely as him except they don't know it, and should be allowed to pretend they're having fun.

* * *

And there are boundary markers in the lawn, these thin iron rods like bridge cables twisted around that stick up out of the ground maybe a few inches, must've been put there after the war when the neighborhood was built and it's strange to think of this whole street empty and the place getting plotted off with these rods in the ground and the first families showing up and the fathers still young but rattled about the war and already drinking.

And when the grass gets real high I always forget those rods're there and I always go over them with the mower and there's that huge crunch and I'm an idiot and I jump up real quick because I'm afraid the blades will break off and they'll fly out at full speed and chop my feet off at the ankles, I've worried about that since I was a kid, it's so silly. And that Saturday I looked around real stupid like my neighbors might see it, but then the pain from that sudden movement shot into my back and I forget the neighbors, nothing's as real as the feeling of splitting like I can't move but the spasm subsided almost right away, and as I righted the mower and started throwing it under the small red trees in the front yard, soft red leaves but low to the ground, I just throw the mower under there blindly since I can't see under it, my phone rings, but I ignore it. I know it's her and she must be ready for me to pick her up but she'll leave a message and I'm almost done and it's always a pain to stop and start again.

There's a t-shirt I always see that makes me feel different, something about a famous surf-shop and all kinds of people you see wearing the shirt, teenagers and old men, and I always wondered what that kind of life must be like. It can't be like the movies but it can't be like having a real job everyday either. I think of myself, already getting older, shirtless on a beach all day with a dark red chest and grey hairs burnt white and starting to wrinkle and if I'm not safe everything starting to sag. Life on the beach, cold sand at night, sandals and boardwalks like when we were younger and couldn't afford to go overseas, all the lights from the t-shirt shops and souvenir joints and what all those lights must look like from out on the water and some missionary group doing a huge sandcarving, of all things, of Jesus and the crucifixion, and handing out tracts. The whole thing of always eating outside or around those bars like pagodas and crowds in a swirl, I think of these people as illiterate even though I know they aren't, or carefree even though I know they aren't, I don't know what I think of them except that they're different from me, that they might be just as paralyzed thinking about my life, or at least what it used to be.

The last guy I saw wearing one of those shirts was a guy who always shipped stuff I was sending out and I got there late one night and he was on his way home and had changed his clothes. He was a nice guy, early forties though he looked younger, face like he must've once been a boxer and he couldn't have been getting paid much to weigh and ship stuff. He wasn't married and I hardly ever heard of him with a girl and he had a crappy job and all he talked about when I saw him was what was on TV last night, he was one of the first people I ever saw actually watching a movie on his phone and I said I'd never do that, said I'd never do a lot of things. But he said one night he was training to be a bartender and I guess it'd pay more but I could tell he wasn't worried about it and I thought of my mortgage and car bill and what the doctor had told me and how we'd been talking about children again, and here was this guy whose whole mind was on becoming a bartender and learning drinks and subbing at places for training, and why shouldn't he, I was happy for him.

* * *

I was almost done cutting the grass, still a twenty foot square looking even higher from how short it was all around, when the phone rang again and I actually sighed and swore as I stopped the mower and stopped the music I was listening to and went to the shade under the awning to answer it, it was some lady she worked with using her phone.

That night somehow when I was able to fall asleep I dreamt as I do all the time of my eighth grade class reunion, I always have, and almost every time even as we're all in our fifties now I dream of us all as twelve-year-olds again, but that night we were older, maybe in our mid-thirties, but still much older than ever before, but in a second it changed into a movie, the camera in the backseat of a cop car and two cops going down a dirt country road and the one in the passenger seat the rookie and the driver a veteran, and the new guy says *Who's that walking on the side of the road?* The old guy tries to tell him it's no big deal, the guy's here all the time, and of course it's me, and I'm as old as I am now and it's only this young cop who prompts the old one to stop the car and he comes up to me and I can only ramble in the heat, since it's summer, about the grade school I graduated from and our reunion and where was everyone, I was lost. And the young guy took my name and the school's name down and the year, like he was going to look it all up and verify it, and when he pointed into town we all saw the humped shape of a dead deer further down the road and its broken body, and the dream must've gone on for awhile after but I can only remember how the smell of the dead deer was coming at us up on the wind.

* * *

At this all-night restaurant once, some place that was proud they went back eighty years and had old menus and funny cartoons everywhere, I saw this withered guy come up to the counter and he had unlaced white tennis shoes on and he shuffled and he had sweatpants on and over that and I don't know if he was shirtless but he had a big green jacket on and all the clothes sagging on him, all of it, his skin even seemed to sag on him and he was bald and it was as if he didn't have the strength to keep his mouth closed or that all of his skin was sliding away so it pulled his mouth open and left his hands shaking and forced his eyes wide open in staring. His open eyes and his open mouth swam around as if he was blind, he was the saddest person I'd ever seen, and on his jacket was a patch for Vietnam that said he was a veteran and a POW, and I realized it would still be decades before all these old veterans died off, all the old pain and all the lost ones with no families all over and still in rehab or counseling for what they did decades ago, and this guy looked like he already was dead and who knows what happened when he'd been a prisoner, who knows if he may have done horrible things over there. And I watched him because no one else seemed to notice or talk to him and how he sipped his coffee and used a spoon later to eat some hash browns and how at one point he forgot what he was doing and spooned hash browns instead of sugar into his coffee but he didn't want to say anything about it and just drank the coffee and then dug for the soaked potatoes with his fingers when the cup was drained.

* * *

She'd been caught somehow in a crowd of graduated students and their families. It wasn't even her job but once a year on a Saturday she went to help and it was held in the same arena as the hockey and basketball games and concerts were and she never went to her own graduation and I think it made up for that, she was always so cynical about so much and I think families being together and old and young people being together and a genuine sense of celebration really meant something to her since it was so rare, she felt so much and that's why I loved her and it was so hard for anything but us to really make her feel good about the world.

And it was a running joke between us because we'd been given free tickets to concerts at that place more than a dozen times over the years and we always took them but in the end always decided to stay home. Of course I see great significance in that now, like our staying home was a sign of what would eventually happen, but it's unimaginable to me that her life and mine with it was leading up to that moment and the only hints we were ever given of it was that we never used free tickets to go to the place, that's not really a world I can conceive of.

Years previous I'd driven to pick her up and always been slow and careful going down that road, clogged with police directing traffic and kids in their caps and gowns and their parents, none of them paying attention and just spilling across the road to the parking lot on the other side, and that day she was with them when someone coming the other way ploughed through and somehow it was only her that died, smashed and then dragged to the next stoplight beneath the truck, some shithead with bumper stickers and a gun rack, and it's stupid but when I saw who'd killed my wife and how he'd dragged her the way he had I said I thought he probably wouldn't think twice mounting her on his fucking wall, just another dead animal for him.

* * *

One of the first jobs I got as a kid was a grocery store and the manager there was in his late thirties, he had kids and a wife and people all said he'd spent time in prison or at least jail and the more I got to know him he talked to me about all that and said how as a kid my age it was a great and a powerful thing to hold a gun on someone. He said he'd never used it and just pointing it at someone was enough, it was enough power since he could take their money and it was what you did when you were that age.

But he was always playing catch-up and his lack of college always bothered him because he thought other people noticed and it bothered them and he always used words in a weird way and he always used his hands when he was talking like he didn't have the words and wanted the hands and the words to mean something really deep. He was a good man but wished he was better and knew that he wasn't, or at least to his standards. He took care of his aging father on the weekends and his kids loved him and he didn't have a lot of money but he dressed as if he was going to his usual courtside seats, or just to a funeral, everyday, like he was the president. I never saw better shoes than his and a way about him like he belonged in the forties somewhere going to baseball games in a jacket and tie or zoot-suit or long hours at a jazz club.

Except he was at a grocery store and he always complained about the customers and the people, because they did treat him horribly—because that's what customers always do—and young kids like me working stock always came in late and even kids in their twenties came in late and he'd ramble on (and complain out loud to me, he trusted me) about how stupid kids were these days, didn't respect a job and didn't realize how lucky they were, all the same stuff. And as if he wanted to be an example to them he came in early every day, come in early every single day and walk the floors like a king dressed up like he was and shaking hands with the stockboys and the cashiers and the deli and bakery people and the regular customers, and I knew even young there was some kind of hole in his life and some kind of problem at home he wouldn't tell anyone about, some stab at class or rank he wanted to live up to.

And even being that young I knew he was better than all of that but he was twenty years old than me and I knew advice from a kid would be an insult, and really thinking about it now it was probably pretty condescending to imagine I could tell him anything. But even still, what did I owe to him? When you see someone in misery is it your duty to tell them so or burst the only safe bubble they might have, like my manager's solace of coming to work a king dressed to the nines, to find a worse misery underneath?

At least the smaller sadness you can deal with.

How was he any better or worse than the old cashier lady, she was retired and working there because she'd never been married and was lonely and she always looked completely beat down and no one talked to her and she wore a plush pin on her vest of a cat sitting in a shoe and the pin was as wrinkled as the rest of her clothes and her sagging arms the bottoms of everything like her hands and legs and face and ears and eyelids that just sagged and I hated to see her, she was so sad. What is our duty to people like that?

I ask myself now because no one seems to be asking it of me. I always dropped every friend when I fell in love with a woman and now there's no one left. I used to fake interview historical people in my head all the time and do huge dialogues of things. Now I interview myself because no one else is asking the questions.

* * *

Before she died I'd spent months and probably years collecting movies and pictures and making these hours-long sets of home movies of travel footage that we'd done since we met. We both admitted, not with false modesty or anything, that we were looking better and better the more we aged because there was no more pressure to be some pretty girl or some dumb boy and none of that anxiety, and so just a woman and just a man of a certain age comfortable in their bodies and able to talk and talk. All the memories saved up that were gone.

Before I'd met her I traveled around a lot and I was aimless and it wasn't until we met that I saw what a waste it'd been before she came around. She'd asked about my friends and people I'd met in all these places I'd been to but I couldn't think of a friend really and I made a list of fifty or more people I'd met up with and talked to at a restaurant and met at a bookstore and a bar or through other people and nearly all of them I only saw once, they were my one time people. And when I made that list I could see them all again and I remember being really happy, but I only saw them once and I never sought them out and they never sought me out. And I don't just mean women, I mean men, I mean couples, older people, anyone.

And when she was killed I found that list again because she'd laminated it as a reminder to me of what she really meant to me, and this time around looking at it I couldn't remember any of them anymore except for a couple I saw out once and then again at a diner and we sat and talked for a few hours, me and single on one side of the table, and the two of them on the other side who were really affectionate and sweet.

But the rest of them are all gone. They've been replaced by others and some nights as I drive or walk or as I take a train or arrive at an airport and don't stop moving I feel a great sense I can't explain of something lifting me up, and as I approach a place filled with lights on the inside and crowded with people and as I approach and understand that she is dead and in the ground, but that I never knew what happened to these other people, to any of the people I've seen and come to know only briefly, I think that in her absence I deserve to walk into a place like this—some perfect diner off some cliché highway—and find them all there, waiting for me, greeting me with the looks not of a stranger, but of an old friend.

Bearing the Names of Many

1

IWILL SIT. I WILL REST. I WILL SLOW DOWN AND SLEEP.

A picture of somebody in their thirties. Disarmed moment, pained or tired. Old t-shirt. One of those old automatic throwaway cameras, so they're caught in this huge flash and the background is washed in dark, burned. I completely fall apart at this.

Because he was a little boy once, grew up, dozens of classrooms and friends, schoolbooks, girls he liked and girlfriends, nights of first anxiety over tests. Joys at things loved, the bedroom redone twenty times before he got older, move out.

We've all been in the second-grade, some version. That's something.

It's impossible to say what I mean. That a disarmed adult photo says all of it, in the eyes. The pain and uncertainty are all still there. And the happiness too. First loves and hates and anger and real joy, music and movies.

Everybody has these, the length and breadth and weight of life behind everyone. Behind every second. Behind every single second, movement, pore, gesture. So full and huge and vast, so deep. Behind absolutely everyone, without question. But since these moments are different for each of us, we don't get along. What airs and arrogance we put on to seem profound, all our distinctions. When we just want that weight. That love and fullness. That complete wholeness.

MY PRIVATE OBSESSIONS AREN'T WORTH MENTIONING. Like someone who cries over a painting or knows something about art or music, or just sports, and can go on and on about it, all the specifics. It's the foundation of their entire life, but on some tragic level totally private. They bring it up in anything like mixed company and nobody knows what they're talking about. It shouldn't be like this, but nearly everything we love are just wedges, they just drive people apart. Drive them away. Because everyone else just has another wedge, another love, millions of them, just as strong. We have no capacity to deal with this. It's so threatening. I want to ask why but it just is.

So I won't go into any of it. You'll be able to guess some of mine, maybe, the things I love that you don't. But it won't matter if you do. What we all loved before last year is useless, before sickness and planes falling out of the sky. And that war everybody's been worried about, finally here.

We need to crowd around something we can all relate to, or we'll end up ripping our throats out, burning to death. Talking about Michelangelo isn't worth that, if it just isolates you, makes you feel better than everybody, or if hearing about it threatens you. Nothing's worth that. Or talking about some baseball team. But I'm sure we'll do that rather than caring.

2

BUNDLES OF NEWSPAPERS STACKED ALL AROUND. Strange with all this technology that stacks of paper are still here. And still tied with those strands of brown twine.

ON THE BUS. Mostly full. Elderly couple next to me. Old man asleep in huge orange sweater. Hearing aid in his left ear. Black hair bursts from behind it. By the sound of his snoring it's all in his nose too.

EVERY MORNING FROM THE WINDOW. And every afternoon coming home. A man sweeps the empty concrete bay of the machine shop. All the dust from the deliveries. Departures. Men smoking all day. Different guys all night. This never ends.

FUNNY, EVEN WHEN NOT IN A HURRY I'M
IMPATIENT IN CARS. But I'm never impatient on the
bus. We're going slow, but so what? Must still feel like a kid,
back seat, you're being driven somewhere and it's not up to
you, and it's fascinating enough just to watch the scenery.

WOMAN ON THE BUS. Tall and in a pea coat.
Holding onto the railing above her. If not for the crush of
people all around she'd never keep her balance. Her eyes wet
with tears. Her cheeks shining awfully with them. When
I first saw her she was still trying to stifle them, biting at
her lips that'd been bitten and purged of lipstick at the
last stop, or the one before. But as the ride continued and
as more people came on and went off, and as no one gave
her a seat and as the commotion of the doors and the stops
and the announcements all continued, she gave up trying
and was only determined to do it softly. As the tears just
poured she closed her eyes and she began to breathe deep
in and deep out. To calm herself down. But she never
calmed. Wish I could kiss her crying eyes. Could ask her
who died, who's going to die, what news from here or far
away has made her this way.

MAN ON A BUS YESTERDAY. I wasn't there but
they're all talking about it. Stood by the bus door and at
a stop suddenly drew a hammer from his coat and started

beating the nearest seated man in the face. And he kept swinging. There's video of it. The newspaper dropped from his hands, the hammer tearing through it, he tried to deflect the hammer with his arm, he tried to kick the man with his feet. He couldn't keep himself from being hit. When he lifted his arms he got hit in the side. When he dropped his arms again, his face and head. And the hammer hit the plastic seats and made a thud and a crack. And with each upswing and each swing down the hammer hit the steel bars above and beside the seats, ringing, ringing, like a bell.

MORE THAN A YEAR SINCE THE PLANES STARTED FALLING OUT OF THE SKY. Another summer. Planes losing radar contact, apparently plummeting like a diver and disappearing into the ocean—when this happens there's only one ocean—and unfound. Or going down in the desert. Or brought down by accident or on purpose in eastern Europe, the airport in Israel, somewhere else. So many planes by now. The reverse of aerial bombings, now civilians being shot out of the sky, from the ground. Or planes filled with disease cases from all over the world and somehow that's how it gets here. No one goes South anymore since that's where they first landed.

I don't know why I go to work anymore. Pretty soon they won't be able to pay us. But none of this is happening as quickly as you'd think, I assume every morning I'll wake up and hear somebody used nukes, some country finally totally lost it and the only reaction from other countries is to do the same. But it hasn't happened yet. As if the end of everything has been waiting around for awhile already, and isn't in a hurry, just outside your door knocking, and waiting a few minutes to knock again, maybe try the doorbell.

MINIVAN ON THE FREEWAY. Back of the window, left side, bumper sticker that says *My Child Performs Random Acts of Kindness to Create a Better World*. Directly opposite, a decal of a kid pissing on the words *Ex-Husband*.

.... 3

OFF THE BUS AND HEADING TO THE HOSPITAL, not paying attention and suddenly see these three guys in suits running straight at me from the other side of the street. I stop and step back but then realize they're just crossing the street, four lanes, and don't want to use the crosswalk and don't apparently want to wait until cars aren't bearing down on them. Running like they're escaping a fire. Running like some hit squad is after them, these round middle-aged guys out of breath once they reach the sidewalk.

GUY IN THE HOSPITAL ELEVATOR. We both get on at ground level, me first. I press Two and stand in the back. He follows behind and presses Two as well. Then presses the Door Close button, rapidly, over and over. When it finally closes he presses the Two button continuously.

The elevator doesn't go any faster, though.

I usually make a point of being the last person off the elevator. I hate how fake-cautious and deferential everybody becomes when the elevator door opens, spluttering and not sure if they should go first, *You please, No really you,* so I just wait in the back for everyone to leave first. But this guy was something else. I knew how to time it just right, since by now he was pressing the Door Open button, and I squeezed by him just as the door slid open. Our shoulders touched. What a shit. Seriously. What a fuck. He was pissed.

I shouldn't have done it. But it made me smile. If he doesn't work here that means he's visiting a patient, someone he loves. But I could tell his rush had nothing to do with mourning or distress. He's just impatient. He won't last long when all this is gone. He's one of the ones who can't understand suicide now, even judges it, but will end up blowing his head off.

WOMAN AT WORK. Mid-forties. Brown hair. Still the highest heels she can manage. Sometimes ones she can't. Stumbles around. Clacking like a fucking tank. Her walk is as loud as the fattest nurse here but she weighs about a third. All because of the dumb shoes. From far away still youthful. Up close just a ton of makeup. Sad face, bags under eyes, lonely look. No eye contact, ever. Skirts and blouses like she's divorced and ready again. Like my wife.

Therapist, or just friends, told her to look pretty, which means look twenty.

I'm not judging her. She's no symbol. Doesn't typify anything. Her life and pain and joys are all completely unique and unknown to me. Private and powerful. I mean, they get her up in the morning. And she just happens to be the one I saw today. She means everything to herself and it's not my business, even feeling sorry for her. Though I do. I feel the same for all women, what they have to put up with. But nobody needs my pity.

LIKE THE OTHER NURSE, MY AGE. Gorgeous. One day some friend of a friend dies and you can see it on her face all day. Everyone else has learned to hide everything. I don't just mean doctors and nurses. Everyone. A breakthrough to real emotion is so impossible, unguarded. Yet she looks like she'll just crumple in a second and cry for days and days. I was so happy to see this, to be that unguarded. It's so rare. I must be a sadist. But this sadness doesn't turn me on but I am drawn to it. Maybe it does turn me on. It gives me hope. I'm so stupid.

4

THE LAST TENDER MEMORY I HAVE OF MY WIFE. My head on her stomach. Her in bed and me half off of it, not ready to sleep. Her hands through my hair, the most comforting thing. Whispered something to me in her tiredness. I nodded and assented to that sound. I agreed to things I didn't understand, just the rhythm, the tone, the lull of her voice and the look on her face I couldn't see but knew was there. The love of that great familiarity, to mumble and know you're heard, and understood.

Wish I hadn't left the room that night. Wish I'd been tired enough to sleep, and hadn't gone to the other room to read, whatever I did. I'd trade anything now to know what dumb everyday thing she was saying to me. It would be like water.

IT IS A RAWNESS LIKE AN OPENED WOUND. A beautifully opened wound. This vulnerability. This hope. This nervous anticipation.

WHO KNOWS BUT THAT SHE IS NOWHERE. No matter how many movies I go to. Diners. Museums. All places I linger in for the wrong reasons. Like when I was twenty and dumped, and went to the same places. I'd hear a woman's voice and turn and look not at her face but at her hand, if someone was holding it, or for a ring. Now all over again, looking for her. Whoever she is. Who knows but that she is nowhere.

I KNOW HOW IT IS TO BECOME USED TO SOMEONE not being around until they're just lost to you.

5

HONESTY HAS ITS PLACE. But it can't be bald. I used to think with my wife or among my friends that simple honesty was enough. It would take care of me. If it was upset, if I was happy, if I was asked a question: simply answer it unadorned. Just bring it up and talk. Getting it out was more important than how I get it out.

But timing matters. Context matters. And coddling. I said once I'll never give a compliment and then mention something I want. I'll never try to coach someone into thinking my idea, which they'd never agree with if it came from me, was actually theirs first. But you have to.

WE ARE SUCH BABIES. Such children. So fragile. So easily broken. So easily broken so completely. The truth is not enough to set you free. And neither is love. Or perhaps knowing that, and living it, is enough. And perhaps that is the best of love. Caution. Care. Understanding. Perhaps what I'd taken for the worst calculation actually is the best of love.

KNEW A GUY ONCE, FOR YEARS WAS ADDICTED TO DRUGS. After he cleaned up he said his son had done that to him, he realized he had someone else to live for. And I didn't tell him, I would never dream of it, but I thought he was full of shit. But I know it's something different now.

I understand what he meant. If the world were different, we would see our worth like waking up, it would be self-evident and we wouldn't need anyone or anything to show it to us. But it's a harder world we have, and we need to take our worth where we can find it, however we can.

SPENT THE DAY WITH MY HEADPHONES IN. Just completely moved. Allowed myself to hum. To drum on my knees. To put my head in my hands. Close my eyes. Grin like a fucking idiot, smile, laugh, nearly cry. I really did almost cry. Somebody would say my name and I'd turn. This happened a few times. And I turned around and whatever look I had on my face made them step back, either in their eyes or actually with their feet. I've been floating all day. I can't imagine what my face and eyes must have looked like. One of the best days. One of the best ever.

DREAM: BEING SENT OFF BY A CROWD OF PEOPLE, MY PARENTS THERE. To a hotel in some kind of foreign place. Given directions. Getting lost, arriving at the wrong place. Invited in, again amidst a crowd of people. This is another hotel, but in a house, a B&B. In one of the rooms there's a bookshelf with some novels. Later meet with the owner of the house and thank him for having those there, I don't remember the authors.

At some point I ask where something is. Or I'm just wandering the house. End up in the basement, which has a dirt floor. Empty except for the poles that are scattered around like pillars, holding the ceiling up. This underground seems much larger than the entire house above could possibly be. There's a bathtub sitting randomly around. A cheap piece of wood as a wall beside, a mirror there.

I turn around and see a little boy screaming or crying who suddenly grabs hold of his neck just as blood begins pouring out of it. His face squinches up and he disappears. I turn and look in the mirror, terrified, turn and look all around. I turn back to the doorway and look where the boy was. There's something there that scares me even more that I can't remember. A much larger shape.

Can't remember the rest except the general sense that the man who owned the house and all the people in it were all implicated in these things somehow. All sinister. That the little boy wasn't the only one.

6

AFTERNOON. FOUNTAINS BY THE CHAIRS AND TABLES SO WE CAN SIT OUTSIDE. Wonderful when the water starts up just as the wind picks up and a cold spray is sent towards all the serious adults with their serious concerns, all the doctors and nurses. I'm as old as them sure, but that just ain't me. Some get up and leave, their papers wet, their clothes. Others just shiver and laugh, cry out. A great sound that will be gone. It gets my book pages all wet but I love it, I don't care.

AWHILE BACK THE HOSPITAL BROUGHT IN some teacher to give a talk to the physical therapy patients, little kids and war vets and on up to the elderly. Gave a talk about Michelangelo. Haven't been able to forget it. I only listened in because I'd heard Michelangelo had lost his mother when he was really young and I wanted to see what they said about that. I only really know about one or two of his things. Guy said even his best stuff were just excuses to show how the naked human body looked at rest or in motion. And how he ended up doing statues and paintings of people in these impossible poses. Showed a drawing he made where he really finished up one area, the shoulder and back and a lifted arm, but then he left the rest barely a sketch or just not there. That was so nice for me to hear. He spent his life on something so impractical and bizarre as wanting to understand the body, and just so he could represent it himself. What does that even mean? The body is already here. Why bother? It's so wonderful that he did that.

And he left so much unfinished. Those drawings but then there are statues too. Bodies still halfway in stone like they're climbing out. No legs or arms. Or body parts still clinging to the huge backgrounds of stone. Faces and beards and heads still in the block looking up and twisting, only the front of the face or the side of the head carved. The rest uncarved, still a blank. The guy said that for many people and maybe even Michelangelo himself that these half-finished statues hold more meaning than his finished ones. And this made everyone, especially the little kids on crutches, smile somehow.

OVERHEARD IN THE CAFETERIA. Guy in his thirties and guy in his twenties.

Twenties guy, after describing some date he'd had with an older woman the night before and how he didn't think he needed to tell his girlfriend of a year or so, asked if that counted as cheating. *It's not like we're married or anything.*

Thirties guy, a little stunned and apparently wondering why the question was being put to him, says, *Well, the best way to answer that is to ask yourself how you'd feel if she did the same thing to you.*

And if you could've seen the younger guy's face. Seriously. It just fucking fell. Amazed at the suggestion and just floored at the thought of this being done to him. But still not caring about his girlfriend. This whole reaction just about thinking of her doing it to him.

How it is you spend a year with someone and still lack all ability for empathy is beyond me. How that very thought never crossed his mind is completely beyond me. I'd respect him more if he'd had the thought and still cheated, at least he'd be aware.

I've done some terrible things but I at least knew it as I did them and felt guilt from then on. Still do. How guys like this (and large numbers of them) will exist soon is beyond me. Completely guiltless. Cannot think of another's perspective. And I don't even mean someone you hate! Can't even identify with someone you supposedly love. Beyond me.

7

HOMELESS MAN SLOUCHED BESIDE A BUILDING ACROSS THE STREET. Hard to even see him there. Car drives up and driver gets out, leaving his car idling in the road. The street is one-way narrow so it's only a minute before another car pulls up. Honking. Honking. Laying on the horn for this guy to get his car out of the way. *Trying to help the homeless guy*, he turns around and says, *I'm trying to help this man.* The other driver honks his horn again and says, *I don't care!* And the first one says, sarcastic, *I can see that!* And that does it. The second one just launches into something. Leaned over his seat to the passenger window, *Don't you guilt trip me like you're better than me, you don't know me,* and on and on and on. All the yelling. The homeless guy, with heatstroke or something, wearing an old sportcoat with his chest bared, just bewildered.

NOBODY IS WITHOUT A PHONE OR A CELLPHONE. Even now. No one crosses the street without listening to something or watching something or talking to somebody.

There is no possible chance of breaking through. Even if I found a way to talk to strangers there would be no one to listen. Nothing I could possibly say could be as exciting as what they're already listening to, who they're already talking to, every possible thing they can already be watching, downloading.

EVEN THE BUS DRIVER! Even the school bus-driver. The light turned green but she hasn't noticed because her face is in her fucking phone.

WE'VE COMBINED TOO MANY THINGS. Auto gardens. Cellphone forests. Leather soil. Tree tires. Trunk graves. Airbag leaves. Antenna stems. Reclining seat hedges. Hibernation mirrors. Remote keyless-entry salvation. Laminated souls. Obsolete squirrel with 256 memory. Standardized-test teenagers. Alcoholic universities. The many drugs of adulthood. Fad prophets. Fad frenzies. Filtered news. Televised mourning. Flashy tragedies followed by sexy commercials. Focused weeping. Twenty-four hour coverage of intense outpouring. Machinery nature. But soon, nets and webs no more. No more chrome-noses on my bumper, tailgating me. No more swerving. No more hours and hours of stop-and-go steel.

AM NOT KIDDING. Not making this up. Mother goes to work last week and then drives to the daycare at night to pick her kid up. Daycare says the kid was never dropped off in the morning. Turns out she forgot to drop the kid off, left it in the car, it died in the backseat. Or in one of the backseats, since it was some huge ten-seat boat that was oh so necessary for her fucking life. Can't even park the thing probably. Can't even drive it around. You pull down a lane in the parking lot and she's coming towards you in the middle of the lane because she can't drive it. Has to climb into it. And so she drove around that day with her fucking kid dead in the back.

BY THE FOUNTAINS. Woman, sunburned beyond her years. Wrinkled beyond her age. Probably meth or something. With an infant on her lap. Her elbow on the baby's shoulder, the crooked arm holding a cigarette. The smoke trailing over the baby's head as if he were some giant infant set down in some metropolis, his head in the smog.

.... 8

ALL WE DO IS MAKE A VIRTUE OF NECESSITY. If we can't change it, death, illness, accident, divorce, scratched car, cat breaks your glasses, it's all made into some possible good. There's no other option. We can't face an unchangeable horror, something that doesn't meaning anything, so we make everything have at least some meaning. Even God's will, to everything. Everything is God's will, no matter what happens. You get cancer, God's will. You die of cancer, God's will. You survive cancer, God's will. What does that even mean.

Or if people die by firing squad or in trenches or death pits, but if one of them survives, or if years later statesmen meet to commemorate what should never have happened anyway, somehow that's supposed to lessen it. *Something good came of it.* Bullshit. Guy has his head cut off on a video. How many of those have we seen by now. Kidnapped and made an example of. No sense there. No justice for him. No kind words will make up for it. Yes, *Now we know about death pits and decapitations, let us mourn.* It supposedly means something to us. But means nothing to him. He died unjustly and there's no changing that. Or making it better. The pain of your head being carved off. The pain of a pit filled with your family and friends shot in front of you with hundreds of others and you about to be with them. There's nothing for them. Nothing for that. Nothing. Isn't that something to realize? *Nothing.* Absolutely nothing. Nothing can take that moment of injustice away, even if on the other side there really is some loving God.

Because people aren't symbols. There's no justice there. No meaning. No meaning, dying a death one doesn't deserve. And so much of our lives is just what we do not deserve, so much is just what no one ever deserved. I need to remember this as I go. As I go I don't know where. No evil or brutality is punished as much as it deserves. And the darkest things cannot be undone. Cannot be made good or right. There is no redemption from a death pit. These things are immovable pillars. The most we can do is try to build different pillars. More numerous and more strong. As I go, wherever I go, there will only be giving.

And another thing: an end of false emotion. Commemoration. No false weight given to them. God and love and empathy, yes. But also atrocity. Also complete horror. Face it. Face it: back of a transport truck and your four-year-old kid won't be quiet. So the truck stops and the guy with the gun comes around and grabs him by his feet and swings him and explodes his head on the side of the truck, throws the body on the ground. Laughs at the mother. Or just ignores her. That. That. Over and over. History. That's history. And nothing makes up for that. Ever.

THIS IS BASICALLY CHILDISH STUFF. I realize that. Everything's going down and I'm wondering why things are the way they are. Why joy is so impossible without pain. Disappointment. Sweat. The people who succeed with money or art or politics only do so by driving themselves crazy. Michelangelo in a letter, says something like, *Only distraction prevents you from being beside yourself with grief, just please write back to me about something, I don't care, anything.* For normal people it's the simple truth of just keeping busy, keeping busy, keeping busy. Everyone says that. *Keep busy, otherwise you'll think too much.* Because if you think too much you'll obsess over something and go crazy over that. So, at least be minimally functional rather than going crazy over something that isn't practical.

Why is that? Why the fuck is that? Honestly. That we have to distract ourselves with busyness so we don't think too much? Why should thoughts and feelings be so powerful and so unwieldy? Why are things that way? It's not a good arrangement. If I were God I wouldn't have done it that way. Minds, religions, hearts, all stacking the deck against us, over and over. Down to some dumb actor who says he won't do movies anymore unless he's terrified and scared to go to work everyday, something really extreme. Why is something that isn't extreme considered either distracting or just boring? Why is calm so uninspiring?

Yeah, and I wonder what that actor's thinking now, with movies not a thing pretty soon. Am I just being childish? An idealist?

THIS IS WHY I LIKE WORKING WITH COPIERS. Could just as easily have been with cars. Building bookcases. Fixing bathtubs. Completely mechanical and obvious. Something's broken, move this piece. Replace that one. Do this or that and for sure it will work. A million different possible problems. But for all of them a clear and concise and definite answer. Not this vague unanswerable childish bullshit.

BECAUSE I'M STILL JUST A LITTLE BOY. A little boy with his stories. My favorite one as a teenager was me dying in a car crash in the rain. Usually just after somebody dumped me. Like, *She can kiss my ass, now I'm fucking dead, how do you feel now.* And how as the paramedics came and just as I died, I would tell them to tell her that I still loved her. And in this fantasy I could think about how she would live the rest of her life guilty, or just moved, or just paused for a moment, missing me or feeling for me.

And you know how pathetic I am? I imagined all of that again when my wife left. I thought that same scenario *yesterday*, more than half a lifetime later, with the benefit of an education and forty years on this earth to teach me more than enough. And I sit here in an empty apartment surrounded by all of history. All of literature. All these books. All these ways of dealing realistically and wisely and well with all the difficulty and with all the pain and sorrow of life. The lives of noble men and women and everyday people everywhere. From zero to Sumer, and Sumer to now. Lessons everywhere. And my only thoughts sometimes are about dying melodramatically. And as I die, I'm sure, I'll run her name together with all the others. My friends and all. Mother dead ages ago. Father a few years after. Tell them I love them. What a crock. I'm so pathetic.

Because at eighteen I knew that was an illusion. I knew even then that in reality dramatic deaths never happen. And now I know even better how most things actually run out. Or, they don't run out. They just go on. I'd more likely just run into her (whoever she was) in a grocery store. In the park. In traffic. And we'd both just still be alive. She wouldn't be brooding over me. Not missing me. Not even thinking about me. She'd just gone on. And so had I. No last grand gestures.

And the same here. The same even in this completely other world that's coming. Might run into her in some camp months from now. Some crowd years from now. Or not. Just not, just fucking not. Even now, life will just go on without my ever having said what I meant to say to her, to anybody. Without ever meaning anything to anyone.

And that is all. No vestige of a beginning, no prospect of an end. No lie from fiction. No great organization of scattered experiences to equal a narrative. No false symbols. No phony significance. No false meaning. None of that bullshit, anymore. No beginning, no middle, no end, no closure.

BECAUSE WE ALL HAVE CHILDISH DREAMS. Fame. Money. Power. Position. But hardly any of them pan out. And hardly any of them are worth panning out. And anyway, hardly any of us will ever decide upon a new law or the dropping of a bomb or even a trade between two teams. But it's what we all want. Always some great outer thing we can be recognized for.

But outside the realm of a few hundred politicians and

a few hundred businessmen or team owners, the only lives in most people's hands are our own and those closest to us. And that is paralyzing, that knowledge. Knowing what real power is, that kind of power. And what anonymous power it is, that kind of anonymity. And along with the knowledge that it's not what we've been told to aspire to, it's not what any of us ever wanted, it's too hard.

So we screw it up. Our own lives or somebody else's. And no fame follows. No media attends to a sad house. No opinions on politics or bands or anything helps. Nothing assuages the slow rending private unraveling. All of it is unseen and without image and nearly wordless beyond the front door. Unless you make a fool and gossip of yourself.

Which again, despite the worst examples from TV, most of us never actually do. So that the real life of being alive, is the real pain that only exists because of the real joy. It leaves no trace in the world's history except in our memory. The good and the bad. Because this isn't all bad. But the realization of it can't help but be bad. The paralysis of it. It all seems too massive to just be between us, our entire lives, only between two or three people and without them utterly forgotten. It seems too massive to be forgotten so easily, too massive and huge to be so frail, too massive to be our responsibility entirely, and to never be recognized for it. It can't be that way. And yet it is.

9

Two men in their sixties, talking about their grandchildren.

First one, new grandfather: When you have them yourself, you're so busy with it, you can't enjoy it, it's so different now.

Second one, a grandfather for a long time already: You really have the time to stop and notice, see everything.

First: I can put her on the floor, no kidding, just put her on the floor and just watch her for hours, noises she makes, how she moves, it's so interesting. I don't remember that the first time around.

Second: I even say, it's not that I love them, my grandchildren, but that I'm in love with them. I love to see them, hear them, talk to them, hear what they have to say. I can't wait to see them—

First: That's it—

Second: There's nothing like it.

How many of these grandchildren will survive? How many of these grandchildren will grow up in anything like a recognizable world? Half our young men have been gone more than a year already, they'll never know their fathers. How many of these grandchildren will ever know their grandparents, will ever understand generations, and passing-down, and the gifts of old age? Even dumb clichés like *Respect your elders?* And so how long for all that to come back once it's gone, some great re-awareness of time and the old people who with their age are keeping it?

CAME UP FROM THE LAUNDRY ROOM WITH A FAMILY ON THE SAME FLOOR. Little girl, Sunday dress, curls. She ran and giggled and kept looking back to make sure they were still there. She laughed and ran to their door in that way children do. Chasing after nothing. Or some imaginary thing. Not needing an excuse or reason needed to laugh and run.

OLD MEN PLAYING CHESS IN THE PARK. Suddenly erupt in laughter, the two playing and the four waiting their turn, all six of them just suddenly losing it. They laughed aloud to each other in a way that's so rare. These men laughed in an almost private way, old men who didn't care if they were being watched or listened to, this while the laughter and awareness of nearly everyone else is the product of being on stage, of wanting but worrying at being watched.

BUS STOPPED AT A RED LIGHT. In front of a machine shop. Early morning. Man standing in one of the front windows. Blue factory shirt and dark blue pants. Cup of coffee in one hand. Staring out at traffic. Maybe in his fifties, standing where the receptionist and all the suits have their offices. But his place is in the back with the machines. The grime. All the noise.

And I felt for him there as I feel for all of them. How many mornings has he stood there? Was this his first job out of high school, thirty years ago? How many years has he arrived before sunrise and watched traffic with his coffee, before settling to his day?

10

COUPLE AT DINER JUST PARTED. The guy has huge teeth and a strange face, and approached and bent to kiss her. A kind of non-kiss. Avoiding the tongue. She seemed to want more and at least kissed his neck. Or maybe whispered something in his ear.

LITTLE KID AT THE DINER. Wanted to win something out of the claw game by the door. He asks me if I have any quarters. I say no. Looking back at the register and then to me he shrugs and says, *Have any singles?*

JUST SORT OF WATCHING THIS WOMAN. Wish she were alone, but she's sitting with some schmuck. I watch her reflection in the window. Instinct says a first date maybe, they don't seem too familiar. (Not sure what the point of first dates are anymore.) She leans on her palm and listens and stares at him and suddenly she smiles and I just want to fall apart.

LITTLE GIRL AT DINER. Mother tells her to apologize for something. Scrunches her face up and crosses her arms and says, *I already apologized, you mean I have to apologize again?*

STILL IN THE DINER. Guy comes in suddenly to a girl at the table nearby. Greets her with a box. He smiles and steps away as she opens it. A white hat. And she bounds up from her seat and just hugs him wonderfully, *Thank you—it's beautiful!* Something she's asked for, something she pointed at while passing a store window. Just some dumb white hat, but it's great, there's a huge history behind it only they know about.

ANGRY SNATCH OF TALK: *SHE'S MESSING around now—she, you know, she called my brother so I left a message on her machine, she's just flaky.*

And keeps talking, out the door.

ANOTHER COUPLE. I'm jealous of them sitting on the same side of the booth. End of their meal and they box up some uneaten pancakes and toast. Then I saw the girl look around and put her own fork in there, and a handful of jelly packets. Before she put the fork in she dipped it in her water and scrubbed it with a napkin and dried it off. They got up to leave and I pretended to go to the bathroom but then followed them outside. Stood by the payphone and watched them give it to a homeless guy who's always hanging out there.

BEEN HERE FOR HOURS. Long enough for the fucking jugglers to show up outside. Or no, it's hacky-sack, juggling with their feet under the light with bean bags. Spin as the bags sink and then kick them with back-kicked legs and feet. Remaining juggled bags fall to the ground as only one is focused on and kicked high up past the window. Over shoulder and body shifts and feet back-kick. Then a forward side-foot kick and back into the air with the lightest or hardest kick. A few feet or many just flying. In the air and back down. Eyes always following.

.... 11

AFTER THE RAIN PASSES AND PUDDLES LIE IN the road in long narrow pools the children appear up and down the sidewalk and wait for cars to pass and splash them. These kids appear every few miles like small adults waiting for the bus. Some wearing no more than shorts. Their hands up hopefully as you drive by. They're already drenched. Their bare feet no doubt dotted with pebbles and mud. I remember the swimming pools and the wet sidewalk summers, eight and nine and ten years old.

CHILDHOOD: WAKING UP IN THE MORNING during winter. The room filled with white. Window-shade up. Snow-covered front-lawn just bursting with its brightness into the room.

CHILDHOOD: I REMEMBER BULGING SCREEN-doors that broke as we ran through them.

CHILDHOOD: PLAYING BASKETBALL BEFORE school started, dew still on the grass beyond the parking lot, so if you missed a shot or it rolled the wrong way it slid into the grass and was all slippery when you picked it up. No way to dry it, except with your untucked shirt.

MEMORY, CHILDHOOD: BENEATH BICYCLES the road trembles and sighs and breathes. Birds on the sidewalk ahead scatter.

CHILDHOOD: THE BRICK SIDE OF THE CATHOLIC SCHOOL. I played catch with the brick. Fielding and pitching with the tennis ball. Threw high or low, soft or hard against the wall and took every position. Shortstop, outfielder, third base. That was me. Hours and hours of imagination and sweat. Whipping it against the brick wall and fielding it quickly again and again. I was not of this world.

CHILDHOOD, BASEBALL GAMES: SHORTSTOP.
Pacing between second and third base. Would clap the
mitt open and closed in between pitches. In anticipation.
Fidgety in my spikes. The moments between pitches and
the world frozen.

IT WAS AN EXCUSE FOR MY WIFE TO LEAVE.
She knew she would never have kids with me, and if she was
going to have them at all, she better find somebody else,
there wasn't much time left. For all I know she wanted to
leave me anyway long before then, and to have the perfect
excuse made up wanting a kid. By the end I barely knew her.

When we finally declared war, I went for a swim. This
was already months after she'd left and apparently found
someone who wanted to be a father, and when we fought I
always joked that maybe she should at least wait until we
declare war. So when we finally did she had the heart to
feel nostalgic and concerned, and I returned her call when
I got home. Said I'd gone for a swim, said it reminded me
of Mother's Day twenty years before. The first Mother's
Day I spent away from home when I lived in the South. I
went down to the river in the rain and swung from a vine
and on the swing back I fell in the water, couldn't get my
feet on the ground.

And she shut me up, *Didn't you hear about the war?* I

said that's why I went for a swim. That's something war won't change, wherever it comes or goes. Unless the water becomes poisoned. Or the rivers glutted with dead, coffins downriver. Which is to say—rivers and clean water are something war always changes! All the more reason for one last spring day. Naked in the water, water so clean I could see my toes.

DREAMT OF THE TWO OF US ARGUING. Completely intractable. Hateful. Just spewing, vile. No attempt at communication or at reason. Or even making a point. Or having the last word, being right. Just hate. Throwing things. But when I woke up I wished it had been true. I would take the worst of that over this.

12

GUY OUTSIDE DURING LUNCH. Some silly ice-cream social thing sponsored by the hospital. So now there're nurses and doctors loitering around outside with ice-cream sandwiches. Nobody makes new friends though, just loiter in the same packs.

Somehow this homeless guy got an ice-cream sandwich. Ratty clothes. I could smell the piss downwind yards away. Now he's sitting at a table nearby, violently going through a newspaper, probably from last week. Could be from the

1940s for all he cares. Coughs violently at regular inter-
vals. Nobody looks at him. Like, *If he wants attention he's
going to have to check in.*

Because sometimes you just want to eat an ice-cream
sandwich in peace. But he keeps coughing at the newspaper,
reminding me that he exists.

THEY'VE BEEN REMODELING ONE OF THE
hospital entrances, so the guard station and the entrance I
usually go in by have been moved. And the guard there is
nearly elderly. Spindly and looking exhausted from some
unknown but eventful past. Now he's forced to sit not at
his usual desk and cushioned chair but high up in some
crappy barstool behind a makeshift desk, looks like it was
made out of plywood. If he looked sad before he looks
miserable now. He can't even slouch like usual.

OLD MAN IN STUBBORN WHEELCHAIR. With
an Army or Marines hat on, must be Korea. Now can
hardly move himself. Hunched in his crappy chair. His
poor wife, also weak, can't get it through the doors. I help
when I see them, try to push then pull the chair over the
threshold, over the bump and the track for the automated
doors. Like I do a cart of copy paper, gathering momentum
to pull towards a speed bump and over. But this is an old
man, and I hated to jostle him. The wife was so thankful.
He looked up at me and I couldn't tell what he thought.

13

THE CLICHÉ ISN'T ENTIRELY TRUE. Not everybody has been running back to religion. But those that have are louder than ever. I shouldn't take so much joy from it but I do love the looks on their faces when I say I'm neither here nor there on God.

It would be easier if I were militantly against them. They only understand extremes. I try and tell them why and it's useless. I say something like, *I don't think religion is what you think it is.* I say, if God is the kind of guy you make him out to be, it's odd we only discovered the germ theory of disease relatively recently. It seems that knowledge of that kind would've been important earlier. That just gets me confused looks. Even laughs. What I mean is that the kind of they God believe in wears a human face and does human things. He acts in the world and allows death and suffering according to a logic and a reason that will only supposedly become clear after we're dead, and so in the meantime we simply have to trust it.

What I mean is muddled because there aren't words enough for it. And no certainty. And that's it. It's assumed there is certainty and justice and fairness that this God dispenses, even though history is filled with doubt and pain surrounding just that fact. But if there is a God it seems to be one that wants us to see virtue in uncertainty.

In a lack of clarity. Because there is nothing but uncertainty. And even more: if this is God, it seems the germ theory of disease and so much else weren't discovered until recently because life is something else than bodily health and perfection. Bad things happen not because they are mysteries of a God's will or just moments when some God is looking somewhere else but because life has nothing to do with certainty or safety or being kept from harm, or of knowing much of anything at all.

What God seems to be about is the best example we have of not having answers. Because in such a precarious world the only option left to us is to care for people as people. Religion is primarily ethical but not in the way they usually mean it. Not because a revelation says so or because a God has decreed it, but because the experience of life negates such decrees or revelations, and our only choice is humility, and is perhaps being decent. Empathy. Identification. Because no one can tell us otherwise, about anything. Religion as it is now is just all a runaround to make us give a shit about each other. But since I give a shit anyway, putting it through that filter is a waste. I won't do it.

14

DINER. A YOUNG WAITRESS AND A MIDDLE-AGED ONE.

Younger one, as she emptied a tub of something, butter or sour cream or coleslaw into a larger tub: I'm too old for this.

Older one: You just turned eighteen. I've been doing this since I was eighteen. And then she added from the kitchen: And my mother's *still* doing it.

OLDER WOMAN. On her way out the door. On the phone probably with her daughter. Loud: That's alright. I think I've either lost one of my lipsticks or washed one of my lipsticks. I can't find them anywhere. You know honey, now you know something that I need for Christmas. Get me a gift certificate or something, you're always asking.

OUTSIDE THE DINER. They play guitar on the other side of the window. Jumping fingers and drumming feet jamming so tremendously. But making no noise to me. It's fascinating. I can't read lips so I make up lyrics to the music I imagine they're making, the beat I can at least sort of approximate, watching the feet.

Diner. Two women, late twenties:

This really hot guy was outside smoking, and whatever I'm not going to come on to him, but I could at least watch him.

Yeah?

So he was talking to his friend and says something like, They're coming to take all our guns, They just are, so they can control us—

Hah! And who's this Them? It's always just Them—

I know. And he just says, I'd carry my gun here but I can't, not allowed, even now not allowed, I don't know why. *I was so disappointed, I just wanted to say, just shut up and look pretty, I just wanted to look at this hot guy and then he had to open his mouth.*

I almost joined in their conversation because it's so true. Those people are so in love with the idea of martyrdom. So in love with being terrified and paranoid and beset by foreigners or anybody. So in love with being afraid of anything or everything, I mean I understand defending yourself but I don't understand your God and your only love and your only source of pride being a fucking gun.

So when the violence they've feared for so long finally does come, it's them that'll actually be the best monsters, the ones now who are so sure that I or someone else wants to take away their dumb guns. They'll love the killing so much, when it comes, when it starts. Some anonymous conspiratorial *They* shadow government, if it ever existed, will be long gone by then, and the only people taking guns and lives will be these dipshits.

DINER. GIRL TO HER FRIEND: *MY BOYFRIEND recently moved out of state. Said he had to get his stuff from his ex-fiancé. But the next time he called me he was in a different state than he originally told me he was going to be in. Now he's talking about getting a job for a year in a completely different state. I've broken up with him but we can't seem to stop calling each other. I thought we were closer and that he really loved me, but I don't know why he's changing his mind constantly. The last time we argued, he said he just wants to be left alone. Then he called me three times. Why do men get involved in relationships if they're not serious? He's way older than me. Wouldn't an older guy be ready to get serious?*

I can't believe these conversations are still happening. I can't believe that women are still wasting their time with stupid men and that men are still wasting their time with stupid women. I would've thought that the proximity of death, or just of everything falling apart, would have made everyone supremely brave, if not in the face of violence at least when it comes to love, to just take chance after chance after chance until something works. But then, of course, I haven't braved anything, I'd rather write this than approach anyone.

DINER. DRUNKS FROM THE BAR ACROSS THE STREET STUMBLING IN. Don't even have to get in their cars. Just stumble from the front door, through the parking lot, somehow make it across a two-lane road in the middle of the night (it's a lot funnier to see in winter), and to the diner and inside. Ordering these huge breakfasts they won't eat much of. Sitting around the circular tables or huge booths. Still loud drunk and funny drunk and groping drunk. Great joy in their friendship. People who've known each other since grade school.

GIRL JUST STUMBLING IN FROM THE BAR. Alone. A law student. I know that because she's yelling about it, telling everybody. Small, skinny, frail. Has some condition. Can tell she doesn't get out much and is wearing clothes she'd usually never wear. Ugly. Bony. Trying too hard. And as desperate as me but just making it obvious. Thinks the end is nearer and nearer. Just wants sex. Or just a kiss. To fall asleep with someone genuinely holding her. I don't know. I feel so bad for her. I've at least known love. The physical excess. The immense giving, crazy fearlessness. The absolutely insane joy and trust of being naked with someone and owning their body and mind as they own yours, betrayal and humiliation completely possible at every moment but the trust and joy and knowledge that, actually, with this person it isn't possible, it won't happen. Or, just walls of photos. She'll never know any of it. Not her. And the way things are she never will, and she knows it. You can tell.

ANOTHER GIRL JUST OUT FROM THE BAR WITH HER OTHER GIRLFRIENDS. Not exactly what they were all saying but it might as well have been: I fucked him. I need that. I fucked that. I need him. But I'm so fucking fat. But I'm so fucking ugly. But I'll have to fucking lose weight so I can fuck him. I love to fuck. It's so fucking liberating. It's so fucking fun.

THE COOKS OR SOMEBODY ARE TAKING A

BREAK, SITTING IN THE BACK OF THE DINER.
The whole middle of the night crush still going on, the
noise nearly unbearable. But I swear he's staring at me.
Don't even know how he sees me, and I'm not making any
noise. Sitting with another guy, white t-shirt, grey goatee.
A few other hopeless guys, and a woman, forgotten people,
clustered in that corner. Hobbling, shaking heads, in the
corner away from everyone. I don't know why they would
be looking at me.

15

WHEN I WAS LITTLE I DREW UP ENTIRE SCORE-
BOOKS FOR VIDEO GAME BASEBALL. I kept all the
stats. I followed players though a shortened season. (The
earliest video games only allowed for thirty game seasons.)
Then the games got better. Real players, full seasons, and
they kept all the stats for you. It was the coolest thing.
They did it for you, it was like the real thing.

NOW I'M LIKE AN OLD MAN. I can't believe
what that's become. We're utterly powerless in the face of
all the information they keep for us. All the statistics. All
the technology we give ourselves to. It's not like I'd have
more friends if phones and computers didn't exist. But with
them it's an utter certainty. No closeness. No intimacy. If
there were I wouldn't need to write this. No one would

need to write anything.

THE NEW, OR I GUESS IT COULD BE OLD, GAME
FOR KIDS THESE DAYS. It's to choke each other and
pass out, and their friends wake them up. Even better are
the kids who do this by themselves. Real thrill-seekers.
Mother found her daughter dead and slumped against the
dresser, the noose still around her neck. All an accident.
But really. Loneliness like that is not an accident. Even
the teenage type that's so obvious. It's not something new
that nobody ever saw. Including her fucking mother.

OR I SHOULDN'T BE SO HARD. They are as
unhappy as I was as a teenager. The adults who act this way
can go to hell though. They're not miserable anymore, just
selfish. They do just want a thrill, assholes who pay people
to "kidnap" them, whatever. The kid still wants meaning.
The kid is still harsh in the new light of realizing the world
is a mess and nothing they've been told to seek is worth
seeking. And no way of seeing that, realizing this, that
there are simply other things to seek. No way of knowing
yet how beautiful things can really be.

16

MORE AND MORE PEOPLE ARE GOING ON

VACATIONS. Buying new cars. Or just buying what they've always wanted to buy. They put it all on their credit cards and know they'll never have to pay it back. I was waiting for this to start. Guess it serves the credit card companies and the banks right. If you're supposed to go shopping after a disaster, to make yourself feel better, why not go shopping before the disaster? They all wanted us to be in debt, irresponsible, just accumulate and buy and own and envy and buy some more. Well here we are. The most I'll do is just go the diner more often.

AND HOW ABOUT THAT. Now that I think of it: they're everywhere now, and seem so essential, but we've barely had a century of cars and planes. Pretty soon we'll be back to a few months or a year to get across the country. To get across the sea. Or not to Europe at all anymore. Who among the survivors will know how to build a decent ship by hand, or have enough people around to get the supplies to build even one? Let alone a dozen? Our radius has shrunk from outer space to barely a few hundred miles, if that.

And what about everyone that's old enough for college, about to graduate, about to go in? Every guy who's about to propose to his girlfriend or already has, they're planning their wedding? Honeymoon, kids? What about people who've spent years working up whatever ladder? Who've finally attained some position or are still a few years away? Who've spent frugally and squeezed every penny for decades so they'd have a good savings or retirement? Who've planned and aspired to some dream they've finally reached or are still far from, and now will never reach? Soon enough, all of it gone.

17

GUY ON THE NEWS. Left his monster pickup on while getting gas, then went into the gas station to get some food. Came out and the truck was gone. Cars have been getting stolen a lot lately. So he tried to tell people his kid was in the car but everybody knew he was lying and cared even less, it was just his dumb stupid truck.

PEOPLE STILL SELLING CRAP. I love it: old gas station, only the roof still there. The pumps long gone and cracked concrete, but on a busy streetcorner so there's always a stall set up on weekends. Today a handmade sign you can barely read from your car, *New in Stock: Gazing Globes*. This sign attached to a folding table of plastic obelisks at whose top are sparkling globes. For gazing, I suppose. And some dude, doesn't matter who or why or what he's wearing except that he's under an umbrella and has sunglasses on, sits behind the table.

SAME THING. Long gravel driveway. At the beginning by the street is some slouched middle-aged lady in a plaid folding chair. Around her on the gravel and lined up on the lawn by the trees and in the high shoulder grass are two dozen or so shirt racks. Just rolled to the edge of the road. The lady has a table and a handful of tupperware containers in front of her, filled with dollar bills and change. Her table and chair between it all. Oh and the Sunday paper nearly covering her face. Quite a composition. She'll still be sitting there when the fire rolls in.

HOW MANY TIMES HAVE I DRIVEN THESE ROADS? Leading into fall, lines of houses. Political signs from last year still there. Suburban to rural and back. Thousands of lives on some road that say something to me they certainly never intended. They don't know it reminds me of my first nights with a license, first times driving alone, first long nights and the feeling of a road and the sense of not needing to stop. The color of midnight on the blacktop, the backdrop of midnight behind the houses, and sunrise if I drove that long.

And railroad bridges, aren't they beautiful? Covered in graffiti and so out of place, standing like an ancient aqueduct, not even two centuries old.

WENT TO THE COUNTY FAIR LIKE WE USED TO. The good feeling that I knew I would get by remembering when we went there together overrode the dread of actually seeing her there. Which of course I didn't. Saw the potters and the metalsmiths though, and realize their skills aren't so quaint anymore. And ditto the ones canning and jarring, or doing anything homemade or by hand. Walked by the pony rides and had to laugh. A tiny oval track surrounded by a close wooden fence, three ponies in different stages of completing of the track. And on each pony some squirming or screaming or just laughing little kid. The parent on the other side of the fence following along by walking backwards, taking pictures and video neither they or their child will live to see. Or if they live long enough, they'll just have no means of seeing it. And at the end of the track, like a conveyor belt, the kid is lifted off, another is lifted up, and this new one is put down, and around and around again. I imagined taking a peek into the barn or whatever where the ponies were kept at night, and looking at their monthly planners. For the two weeks of the fair, one pony had written: *Bullshit*. The other, more empathic: *Fucking bullshit*. The third, more resigned: *Seriously*. I hope they get to run for a good bit when there's no one around to watch.

.... 18

AT SOME POINT I HAD TO RESIGN MYSELF TO NOT CARING. I'll just be the guy sitting on the trunk of his car in a movie-theater parking lot as crowds come in together, talking to each other and with no reason to be alone. I'll just be the one hearing what people are saying when they get out to their cars, I'll be the one noting each word down like diamonds.

PEOPLE STILL PRETENDING. **Around the** neighborhood and far out from it are plastic sleeves stapled to light poles. Inside the sleeves are missing signs for someone's pet. The photo is so horribly copied you can't tell if it's a dog or a cat. I want to call the number just to say that. But I don't. Much better to let them continue in the world where they might find their cat or their dog, as if anybody cares to even look for it.

THE ONLY WOMAN I WAS REALLY WITH BEFORE MY WIFE SPENT THE LAST MONTH OF OUR RELATIONSHIP MOVING OUT. Looking at ads and on the phone or out with her friends taking tours of apartments. When she finally moved out and then regretted it we met at a mall once and talked.

The problem had been that we never had enough money. She wanted things and wanted to go out all the time, and I was just starting my retreat from things. And the way she left confirmed me in what I'd decided. And I met her and told her that she should go and have fun finding someone to buy her things and take her places. I said I probably wasn't an easy person to be with, but I was absolutely positive she would never find someone to love her as much as I did. But I said it's obvious she doesn't want love, and that's fine, and I meant it, I wasn't being sarcastic at all. Some people really do just want things and not love, and it worth at least knowing which one you are.

I went on and on but that was the idea. And she said I was harsh and mean. And it was always strange to me that what I'd said was mean, but how she'd treated me that last month together, knowing she was breaking my heart and gloating over every detail of every new place she found, was not mean or cruel, but just necessary. I found a way to see it from her point of view and hated her even more for it, but I put forth that effort. But that was impossible for her. It's impossible for most people.

NO, SELFISHNESS AND MEANNESS AND A COMPLETE LACK OF CHARITY DOESN'T SURPRISE ME, BUT IT STILL HURTS. What surprises me are when people are decent. Because the whole thing isn't made for decency. Our whole day, from alarm clock to fake TV news to freeway and traffic and to whatever office. It's so inhuman. It's not about relationships. It's not about people.

From when I was little. From when most people were little, kindergarten classes on up. What were the virtues we were taught to cultivate? Humility. Charity. Selflessness. Decency. But culture, technology, relationships, shit we just do to relax, at best they all just make us more selfish and more bitter and more sad. It's hard for me to think of it for long. Most of humanity, apparently for all of recorded history, have worked a combination of jobs in technology and culture and infrastructure and leisure, and all so that we might experience whatever part of those is not our profession. Because we've been told it will make us happy, even though it doesn't. We are mutually feeding ourselves unhappiness, and are happy to do so.

WE ARE LOVEABLE FOR OUR IMPERFECTIONS. Love means so much more when its opposite is so ubiquitous. But this is ridiculous, how shoddy and imperfect and selfish things are. I try at least to notice something meaningful in the endless imperfections. When I see a new car or a new house I want to understand the kind of human sacrifice that went into building those things, even if they're just being put to horrid use by most people.

KID AT THE HOSPITAL CAFÉ, WITH A LADY MUCH OLDER THAN HIM. Maybe his grandmother. Assume they're here for family. They don't mention anyone though. The old lady finally asks what he's studying in school, and he says, *Business economics*. It's too bad he won't live to be my age, and be fine without his degree is business economics, washed free of ambition, and knowing exactly why.

19

I'VE BEEN MEANING TO MENTION THIS FOR AWHILE. Kurt Cobain said fuck you to anyone who wanted to know about his personal life. But he said that to a journalist. And he kept talking after he said that. Ended up with a documentary, his words paired with sad music and photos of himself and places he'd lived.

But both the *fuck you* and what was done with all of his words are right. Fuck you if you make him or anybody into a prophet or a symbol. As if the names and places from his childhood are more emblematic or meaningful than your own. We were all in the second grade once. I watch that documentary about him over and over. Not because he suffered or meant or articulated anymore than most people, or more than me, but just because he was the one that fame hit, and he's just the one who happened to have something made about him. In another world it could have been anybody. We all deserve that, not because we're special in come cultural way, or some bullshit self-esteem way where everybody gets an award, but because we're all special in some private idiosyncratic way.

Because I wept just as much hearing about my mother's upbringing. As a teenager, giving her high school hell for giving her a detention for not having tennis shoes for gym. I can totally see her, young woman, giving somebody hell.

My father and me and her sudden illness not even yet in her blood or her eyes or her mind. But with the same heart as I came to know. Confronting them and saying plainly that her parents didn't have the money for the shoes and she won't punished for that.

Or her own parents escaping Europe after World War Two hiding in a wall somewhere while everyone in the house was shot. My grandmother. Shuffling to an ethnic Catholic church in the Midwest everyday into her eighties. Don't you dare make her a celebrity or a piece of gossip. But make the video of her. Make one for all of us. Our music and our pictures. We all deserve it.

MY MOTHER USED TO ALWAYS ASK WHY I WAS SO NEGATIVE, WHY WAS I SO SAD. She saw it as some kind of cynicism. That I was unreasonably ungrateful. But I've always been overserious and sad because I know how strong real happiness and real love are. And I implode at how close they are, and how they are so endlessly and cheaply squandered. How the actual giving turns to theft before it has a chance to breathe. Pride to arrogance. Security to fear. I don't mean some whitewashed new age nonsense. I mean hard happiness. Love you've dug the ground for. Realizing it's amazing that anything means anything at all. The gift of that.

I TRIED TO PRAY IN THE MORNINGS AFTER MY WIFE LEFT. I woke earlier than usual. Woke earlier than I ever had, and somehow was able to do it consistently. But instead of praying, now I read or hear about people. Interviews. Diaries. Memories. I almost immediately gravitated towards that. And it wasn't fame or renown or "great" people. Just anybody. I would've heard the biographies of anybody. It was just hearing another voice. Talk radio. And so other people have become my prayers. And if I'm incapable of holding any friendships I can at least connect in this way and note down those moments as I see them everyday.

PEOPLE ARE UNKNOWABLE. I feel so much affection for Kurt Cobain but he'd probably hate me. And he wasn't anybody special anyway. That attention could have fallen on anyone with talent. It just fell on him. He was just in a band that made it really big. That's all. He wasn't any more important than anyone else from Aberdeen, any other young person who wanted out and went to Olympia or Seattle. Or some other version of that in another state, another country. The small town and whatever bigger city.

And he wasn't even any happier or more creative with fame. Or money. He said no one deserved to know his private life. The people who beat him up in high school didn't back away from some aura he had, they couldn't have guessed. There was so halo of future fame. They just called him a faggot.

I thought even someone like Michelangelo would have

it, some happiness, some calm. Blessed by God, the greatest artist ever. He had to be something more. But no. Whining to his dad or his nephew about money. Over-dramatic and complaining. Back-broken from work. It doesn't make you happy, talent or fame. And its opposite doesn't make you happy either, and none of these options equals purity. Or calm. Or anything.

But being anonymous at least is easy. That's why I fix copy machines at a hospital. I can be with people. I can talk to them. Touch them. And that's all I need to do. All I have time for. All I should have time for.

HOW DUMB, *THE SOUND OF THE NINETIES*. Like someone in 1730 nodding, *Oh yes, the sound of the 1710s*. Meaningless to anyone but them then, or scholars now. So much of what we hold so dear, the stitch and glue of our memories, just shoddy. Just some shield, all the categories. Just listen to the damn music.

STARTED TO BURN ALL OF MY THINGS. Thought to do this the night I turned the computer off and began writing this longhand. And I've hesitated long enough. I can't stay much longer. I won't let anyone come upon pictures of me. Or files. Or notes I wrote to her.

I'll carry this diary with me until it's filled but the rest have to go. I read some of the old ones, high school and college. And I'm ranting, or just interested in so many things. At least before I dropped out of college, because then I just became interested in other things. And see, that's it. You can see that so clearly from a distance, that I was interested and obsessed with one or two things then, and a year later it's one or two other things, and each time an old interest drops off the new one feels permanent and unshakable. But I forgot about the other stuff so quick. And then I found something else and forgot about the newer stuff too. And then about that.

We remember so little. The most important things were apparently the things I wrote down, so carefully noting down entire days or weeks or weekends. But I forgot about all of them. What about everything I didn't write down? What I didn't think was important? Looks, glances, conversations, possibilities. Moments that could have been different but I didn't care then and let them pass, pass by? What's the point of living what you'll forget, and forgetting the parts you didn't register anyway?

20

WINTER MEMORY OF HER. When she drove, her hands were cold and she would put one of them in front of the heating vent. Her hand hovered in front of the heater and above the radio while the other drove. The warming hand would make fists to get all the heat. Liquid motions. Like she was playing piano or guitar. The center of my sudden attention. The perfection of her hands. I wanted to take that hand and warm it between my own. Wanted to take that hand and warm it with my breath and lips. And suddenly remembering this, the tears for the months and months she's been gone.

THE LAST TIME WE WERE OUT AS A MARRIED COUPLE WAS SOME RESTAURANT. One last deep talk. At least whole and together for a few more moments. Back to our house, my last time there. Another long talk. The illogic of love. The illogic anymore of our lives working together as we imagined they once would. The weakness of how we rushed in the beginning like we said we wouldn't, only inviting this end. It seemed that way with hindsight, that we invited this very evening from twenty years back.

But then, with it all decided she put on home movies. Movies of her as a little girl. I stayed and watched those home movies and for the last time held her as she cried over her mother and father, what they'd done, how they were, how she could never get past it. Her head down. Wearing corduroy pants. Tears falling there into the grooves. I'd done this a thousand times over her parents, and had never been able to help her. That pain was always still there. Fell asleep in each other's arms on the couch and woke in the middle of the night, dark. I left her still asleep.

Dream I've had for years. I'm at work or with her or with my family and somehow I end up somewhere else. A huge grand old hotel. A mall. An office building. An airport. A destroyed city, maze of rubble. And I always get lost in these complicated places. Corridors. Elevators. Hallways. Passages. Stairwells. Rooms and buildings and floors that bleed into each other. And people who bleed into each other. Motives and faces and all of it circular. I can never get my phone or email to work or anything, and I'm trying to get back to work or back to my wife or back to the party or the reunion. I'm late or will lose my job or somebody's worried. And it's monumentally frustrating and terrifying, to have no way back or out. I've always had this dream. Maybe for twenty years, on and off. I've never understood why. I never find a way back. I always remain lost.

.... **21**

REMEMBER THE DINER IN WINTER. Salt-trucks outside. Seen through the slats in the drapes. The freezing rain on the sidewalk. Streets empty except for these huge shovels on wheels. This great darkness. The snow and rain backlit when it falls by the streetlamps and headlights.

DINER. I MUST LOOK PAINED OR INTROSPEC-

TIVE. Or difficult to approach. I must seem mute.

I WON'T BE LIKE THESE REGULARS. I won't. Lonesome. When I come here it's not because I'm lonely. I go because I have something to do. I go to hear people. To see those regulars. To see the same waitresses. Even if I'm quiet I'm not crouched in self-pity. I don't watch everyone with envy. I don't.

BUT I SHOULD NEVER BE ALONE. Or at least feel alone. Feel that just by sitting outside of a group, that I'm not a part of it. Because I am. I am the heart of every group as much as the most exuberant participant. I am always the luckiest person in the world. To be able to see and feel and be as no one ever has. And the same with the guy in the next booth. And the family in the next one.

WITH HER GONE IT'S ALL I CAN DO. Though we met young my habit of listening and watching was older. Far older. First love.

I WAS BORN TWO WEEKS PREMATURE. My mother was out for a walk. She said I came out early because the next-door neighbor woman got a hold of her on her walk. She was a nice but annoying lady apparently with a car-alarm voice and she never shut up. My mother's water broke soon after that walk. *All because*, she said, *I wanted out and away from that woman.* I've always preferred my own company, I've always preferred quiet.

A COUPLE DRIVING FROM PARKING LOT TO PARKING LOT, THEY'RE NEARLY ALL JUST EMPTY NOW. Blasting the radio and dancing.

.... 22

BUS TO THE HOSPITAL THIS MORNING. A wounded bird lying in the road. Rolling around, unable to move. Bus wide enough to not run it over. When I looked in back I saw all the other cars swerving out of the way. Not sure if this is a good sign or not. Better to put it out of its misery? But these are the same people, me among them, who do the same swerve around the homeless people who crowd the outside of the hospital.

GUY AT WORK. Before all of this started we talked movies. Both of us agreed most were bullshit. Concocted by marketers and lapped up by audiences who were just little marketers themselves. Spoiled and critical and self-referential. All with their opinions. Movies weren't even movies anymore really, they were just long commercials.

The guy at work, his solution were bad-good movies, B-movies. Because they know they're winking. They know they're silly and that's all it should be, some fun. But my solution was to wrack my brains trying to find something actually pure, genuine. A great and terrific life-changing drama. Three hours that tore your eyes apart. You could watch it the rest of your life.

Now neither position matters. At some point there won't be electricity anymore. We won't have any stories to live on, except what we tell each other. Thought I heard someone say once that what we call Greek drama is actually just Athenian drama. All the cities had their own plays, but only the ones from Athens survive. That's a nice thought. When it starts over it'll all just be small. No need to please a billion people anymore.

DREAM. IN MY APARTMENT WHICH WAS NOW TWO FLOORS, OR MY BUILDING NOW HAD APART-MENTS CONNECTED BY ANOTHER STAIRWELL SOMEHOW. Heard my neighbor coming downstairs, young guy. My apartment now a huge studio. I was still in bed and heard his footsteps from all over. Pretended to still be asleep. He came over and covered me with a sheet like I was dead, and walked away.

.... 23

WHEN THE PLANES STARTED GETTING SHOT DOWN THERE WAS THE HELL OF GETTING

NEUTRAL PEOPLE TO THE SITES TO INVESTI-
GATE. This in the middle of a war and in the middle of
a totally compromised crime scene. And after that just
the intimacy of the bodies, getting them home to Europe
or Asia. After awhile this became a regular occurrence,
another passenger jet.

Once on the news they showed the funerals, half the screen
in Europe and the other in Asia. Some feat of technology or
just of mourning or scheduling. But all I could think while
watching these two totally different rituals was that there
were millions of shitheads all over the world condemning
the actions and words of one or the other religion. All we
want is love and belonging but all we can do with oppor-
tunities for it is burn it to death.

ESPECIALLY NOW. With religion becoming
more and more extreme the more desperate it becomes. It
seems we just can't help poisoning religion, and it seems
it will be that way or worse for a long long time. I'm
cynical about it but in the end I think it's better than us.
Religion, I mean. We don't deserve it. The best religion
now is like the best ones we've never heard of. The ones
that can exist without the reformers and missionaries and
millions and millions of terrified. Where it's really and
only about humility and love and empathy. But find me a
religion that's really just about that.

BECAUSE THERE YOU GO. Another desperate

guy from some religion. Holding up their book and saying that if their specific beliefs and stories aren't literally true, then whatever ethics they preach alongside them mean nothing. Especially in such a horrible time as this. So that if they aren't the only right ones, then there's no ethics at all. A great dumb childish pathetic showman. Public religion now is finally what it has always aspired towards, a circus.

24

REMEMBER THE BUS DECADES AGO, COMING BACK FROM THE SOUTH. Young kid, heavy accent in the seat next to me. Said he was going into the army. Told me about it. Even though he must have seen that's the last thing I'd ever do myself. Showed me pictures of his girlfriend, and their child. The pictures of his girlfriend were a bit risqué, in her underwear. Not sure why he showed those to me. But then I thought if I were him those would be the pictures I'd want too.

OF EVERYONE I MET ON THE BUS NO MATTER HOW LITTLE OR HOW MUCH I TALKED TO THEM, I NEVER GOT ANY NAMES. I never have.

MOTHER AND LITTLE BOY AT DINER. Opposite sides of the booth. She's wearing a ring, so her husband must be somewhere else. The boy is squirming and looking around and muttering. He talks to her, to his mother, and keeps looking around. He can't be more than six, maybe four. But her face is in her phone and she doesn't say anything back. Except *Sit down, Yes, Okay*. She's not listening. She won't even look at him. She's actually out to dinner with her phone, she's on a nice romantic date with her phone, and her kid just happened to tag along.

Their food is here and she still holds the phone in hand, fork in the other. Won't look at her own child, who desperately wants to talk to her. Finally she snaps and says, *I'm going to tell daddy how bad you're being*.

I want to kick her in the face. If I'm still around in twenty years it'll be feral neglected shits like this kid that I'll have to fight off, for scraps.

STOPLIGHT. WOMAN OUTSIDE AT A PAYPHONE, YELLING. *I'm on the phone! I'm on the phone—the money's going to run out and I don't have another quarter*. She's at most forty but so wasted. A desperate double of herself that now spends most of her time in an old sweatsuit. Scrounging quarters for a payphone to scream into. *You get the fuck down here now, where am I going to go, and you owe me, you owe me you piece of shit*. As the bus started up her eyes caught mine and her voice rose. Saw me and raised her arm and began to point at the phone. At the ceiling. Through the bars. Desperate for a thousand things.

A HOMELESS GUY. Came around at lunch. Heavyset. I know it's so wrong but I'm always amazed there are any fat homeless people. Starts at the guy next to me, mutters through drugs or fatigue or mental illness, something like *Spare any change?*, although it may have been, *Spare any food?*

And I'm in the center of this spiral. I can see him coming, but I'm too much of a coward to get up and move. Somehow I manage to say *Sorry* when he asks me. I make eye contact. He can tell I'm nearer him than these doctors, and wonders why I won't help.

He goes to another set of tables. A girl with headphones on. He asks and she says *What?*, but doesn't take her headphones off, doesn't look up. She makes him ask three more times before she looks up and I want to hit her. Even if she doesn't hear him she has to smell him, to see him. When she finally takes her headphones off she says no to him, then gathers her things and walks away. I saw her later inside, crying. No one knew what she was talking about. But I did. She kept saying, *We're all going to be like him soon.*

25

PEOPLE ARE COMMITTING SUICIDE ALL OVER THE PLACE. I am enjoying this in part because the people killing themselves were the type, only a year ago, most likely to condemn suicides as evil, as cowards, as cruel to themselves and to their families.

But the ability to empathize with someone who thinks or acts differently is still beyond their reach. Because now, of course, those who want to live in an unknown future world are the cruel ones, they're even sadistic, to want to put themselves or their children through such times. And where once the suicide was the coward, now the one who refuses to kill themselves are cowards. Now the speech runs something like, *They haven't the strength to do what's necessary, while I do.* It's appalling.

A man I knew killed himself a few years ago. He'd been through a ton. Addiction, divorce, never settled. But he had a wonderful daughter. His great joy. Only weeks before he'd professed his love and thanks and pride to his little girl, now twenty-five, on her birthday. And after he killed himself a mutual friend said he was a coward. Cruel. And I lost it on this guy. I said to try to imagine how much pain he must have felt, and how horrible must that pain have been, to be more powerful than all the love he felt for his daughter, for his friends, even for the preservation of his own life? Imagine that pain which allows you to hang yourself by a belt from a doorhandle in your bedroom. Imagine not the overwhelming weakness of this man, but how overwhelming the pain must have been to drive him to do that. And so have some fucking sympathy.

Of course this man didn't. It's much easier to judge than

to imagine that kind of pain. And of course now he's one of the many fathers and mothers that have been found dead by their own hands after they've shot their children.

STUFF I WROTE AS A TEENAGER, I KEPT THIS but now I'll surely burn it: *I want this to be as honest as possible, because this is mainly meant for me and my parents, who I think may be worried about me being suicidal. I know I act the way I think I should, stereotypically, because I don't want to worry anyone, don't want them to know me, or I don't want to know myself. Maybe this isn't good, but I know I'm not the nice, quiet kid everything thinks I am.*

Reading this now, the worst part is that it's just a cliché. I thought what I was feeling was so unique. That I was so alone. But I was crowded on all sides by people who felt the same, and I just had no ability to see it or act on it. To have had friends then would have meant everything, but I hardly ever did.

And only a few years after writing those words, I saw a girl in my class in church one day. Sitting behind me. I was wearing some shirt. Something I liked but I thought she'd think was stupid. Or it was a shirt I'd worn to school two days before on Friday, and I was sure she knew that. I thought she noticed. Would think I was poor or that I smelled, wearing a shirt twice so soon. I thought she cared. I thought she would tell everyone. So I kept my jacket on, and there were no fans in the church and I just died in that nervousness and heat.

I can't explain any of that. And no one else can either. This burial under worries. Why we allow ourselves to suffocate like that.

A YEAR OR PROBABLY MORE AFTER MY MOTHER DIED I EXPLODED AT MY FATHER OVER DINNER. I was stupid. Still a teenager. I'd heard from someone, not even mocking me, that they'd seen my dad talking to a woman. He seemed happy. I don't know what it was, that he'd kept it from me or that he was trying to replace my mother. But I blew up at him and told him what garbage he was. He'd had a horrible upbringing, alcohol and abuse and worse. He thought I didn't know but his brother had told me. And here I go and say I knew all about it and then go and say he's treating me and my dead mother worse than his father ever treated him. If I regret anything, I regret that. No one should be lonely. He and my mom had had me young and I'm about his age now and there's nothing more bitter than this loneliness, that particular flavor and bitterness of loneliness at this age. Teenagers have nothing on this. And he was like me. He didn't yell back. And that was one of the few times I yelled at him. So it completely destroyed him.

That night I had to work. One of my first jobs. At a gas station. And I came downstairs in my dumb uniform and was still hopping mad and nearly out the door when I heard him in the living room sobbing to himself. I don't think he knew I was there. But I could pass to the room behind where he was and out the side door without having to see him. And as I went it struck me how ridiculous the world was. That I was obliged for merely practical and material reasons to leave the house this night of all nights. To not be absent or late because I'd already fucked up the easiest fast food and dishwashing jobs, and I couldn't lose this one. So that I couldn't stay home with my father, my only friend and me his only friend, on what could have been one of the worst but then the best days we ever shared. We could've come so much closer. As it happened I went to work and I never heard about that woman again.

MEMORY: MY FATHER DOING YARDWORK IN THE SUMMER. Spreading mulch around and pulling weeds. Underneath the huge living room window. Looks up and sees our two cats watching him from the edge of the couch that's by the window. One meows at him. The other paws at the window. He reaches his gloved hand up to the window and plays with that one. Says, *You're a maniac, you're really out of your mind, you know that?* He loved those cats.

WINTER MEMORY, ELEVEN OR TWELVE: MY DAD HAS THE DAY OFF AND WHEN I WAKE UP HE ISN'T RELAXING. He's brooming the snow off mom's car. Says breakfast is on the table. I know my mom has been home all day when I come home from practice and find fresh sheets on my bed and an extra comforter for winter. Just before she got sick.

.... 26

THERE'S NO REFERENCE FOR ANY OF THIS. No wolves have swallowed the sun. No one's come down from the sky to judge us. No one (I assume) has appeared in the sea, asleep on a lotus and dreaming a new world. It's going so slow. The fear of primal viciousness is just not true. At least so far.

The freeways still work. Utilities are spotty. Most people still go to work, go out to eat. We'll let it seem normal as long as we can. Until the disease reaches us from one shore and the dead are too dangerous to bury, or until the war comes from the other shore.

I'm totally serious. I'm not mocking anyone. I went to my favorite Mexican place and had fajitas, vegetable ones. And I'm still pretending it matters to only eat locally-sourced meat. You could say we're deluded, cognitive dissonance, the worse it gets the less likely we'll admit it. And I wouldn't have thought this a year ago but I think the habits we've made are actually beautiful. Actually resilient, radiant. They work.

TENEBRAE IS A WORD. It was the caption for a picture from World War Two. Dresden I think. Somehow taken from a height. Surprising because the city in the picture is rubble, and you wonder how somebody even got up that high in skeleton buildings. Ashes. Fires.

And down there in the street were three people. I imagine them going through this dead city. Their coats and faces probably covered in the dirt and the dust of the place. I imagined them telling stories, as the world died around them. Or was already dead. A long eulogy. Somehow, voices become powerful again. Somehow, words made meaningful again. Only after voices and words had been put to every horrible use, all the politics and advertising until everything was just politics and advertising, and finally to self-destruction.

I've every sympathy with the suicide, but even still I love how people just go on. I think I will, too. Though I don't think there will be two friends with me.

27

IF THEY WERE READING EVERY EMAIL, listening in on every phone call, and storing every internet search before, they have to be doing that even more now. If only like a child who's stolen an awesome toy and knows his time with it is limited.

But there can't be enough time left to sift through all of it. To discern some threat. But it's all they know how to do. It's all we citizens know to do. Be scared and anticipate. But when anticipation is reality the best of us will flame out under the taper or be eaten in the streets. Burial to death.

What love then, what's still left, will be quantum. It will be titanic. It will be the greatest love, because love will be the only thing left, the only alternative. Every object so precious.

PEOPLE ARE STARTING TO GET ARRESTED. Mostly for no reason. And both the ones who can survive on very little, or who have the money, are escaping to the woods. But in the country there is the greatest threat of violence. It's empty and no one's looking. The cities are still mostly full. So far the violence and arrests seem orchestrated. But the real punishments come in hiding. In basements. By people who know they're powerless, and who are afraid of being rounded up themselves. Who are petrified of the real end, of no power at all, just desperation.

POLICE ARE GETTING YOUNGER AND YOUNGER. More scared and naïve and on edge. The best are overseas and will never come back.

THE POLICE STARTED USING TEAR GAS A LONG TIME AGO. An unarmed somebody had, no surprise, been killed by a cop. The first of many. And with everything else going on the people exploded. But they got it all on video. All on audio. It was a miraculous bit of premeditation, controlled anger and sane outbursts. All at the police. And all of it documented and all of it all over the news all day. For weeks and months. And it was a bright moment of people standing up and not stopping. Because the police killed more people. Arrested others and arrested journalists just for being there. Came out like army rangers in riot gear and armor and it was all on video. They did it but everybody saw. The Southwest and West getting overrun at the border. The South manacled by disease. And now this violence near the Midwest.

Until. Until the rest came toppling down. Until there were larger worries than an entire state and its neighboring borders going under. Until the ability to get it all on video for the whole world to see became impossible for a hundred reasons. Then they could do it all with impunity, all the old tactics, and more. And now it's only rumors.

MORE KIDS KILLED AT THE BORDERS. Streams of them started north ages ago. Sent by their families who had to stay behind. Immediately the followers of a loving, forgiving and compassionate God began going to where these kids arrived, to yell and scream at the busloads.

Along with everything else going on it didn't take long for the protest to become violent. For the places where the buses were sent to become targeted. For the buses to be attacked, the children beaten, for somebody to blow up a bus. This is what was demanded by that loving, compassionate God, and by his spoiled and paranoid believers and their country of immigrants. Even though if they were desperate themselves and even though in another life they wouldn't hesitate to do the same for their own children. And pretty soon they will be that desperate.

Because that's it. They can't imagine being anything but what they are. And they can't imagine somebody else being anything but completely alien. Completely different. No imagination. No empathy. Retreat into the rule of some pretend law. Still asking who's going to pay for it and not how they can help the living. Just help the living.

THE GROCERY-STORE PARKING LOT. Should be a busy Friday night. Just a few cars and the whole lot strewn with shopping-carts. The place already looks like a ghost. The lamps that light the parking lot are still on, I'm not sure how or why. Shining down on nothing. I wonder which holiday display will be left up in the grocery stores when deliveries stop coming in. When they're left to looting. Only then, it won't be called looting anymore. I hope it's Halloween. Free costumes and all that candy for the road.

28

GIRL IN BUS-STATION. Going somewhere far away, for good. Previously reading a novel, now flustered and going over something in a three-ring binder. Going through sheets of paper. All of her bags. Writing something. Adjusting her glasses. Scratching her nose with her glasses. Fingers move over the page with a tight-clutched caution. Perhaps just trying to write neatly. Looks like she could be a prude. Looks absurd with an enormous purse, a bowling ball could fit in there. Introverted. Quiet. Is she crying? A quivering lip whenever she stops to look up. I smile now just as I think she saw me looking. I have to not be so blatant. She sips a drink occasionally. Probably never see her again. Final. I like to imagine she is a mirror. What would people think if they spied on me, glanced at me over their books? But there's no basis for any relationship, as if *Oh, she's just like me.* She could be perfectly aware and happy and not lonely at all. I empathize with her because she's there.

OVERHEARD VOICE IN THE CAFETERIA TODAY, TWO GUYS: WIFE CALLED AND SAID SHE WAS GOING TO A FUNERAL. *Did you hear about that guy who jumped off the bridge?* She used to date him back in college. Actually that's who she dated before she met me. And she says, *Is that okay, to go to his funeral?* And I said *Well, he's dead and we're married and we have kids, looks like I won.*

Though it wasn't quite as nasty as that sounds.

ACROSS THE STREET LAST NIGHT. **Makes no** sense. Ambulance pulls up, lady gets out, talks to whoever owns the house. Then a firetruck shows up. Then another. A third. Another emergency vehicle just down the street, all with lights flashing. A pickup truck from the power company pulls in, guy gets out and talks to the firemen, and the pickup goes in reverse since there's not enough room to turn around, and is gone. Firemen milling around, neighbors by now in their driveways, afraid to ask what's wrong. And then? They all pull out and are gone. One by one they leave. I have no idea why.

STREET FAIR NEAR MY APARTMENT. **Had to** walk through them to get home. Slower and slower as I got closer, the sounds became louder and more massive. Sidewalks up and down crowded with close-packed people in costumes. For every one or two adults, twice as many kids. Faces painted and bodies done up with capes or plastic wings or princess crowns or fake swords or guns. Parents just with burgers in their hands, beer or cigars or cigarettes, or monstrous hotdogs covered in every relish and poured over with ketchup or mustard. Between their bent heads and their shoulders they held their phones and tried to speak to anybody but always failed with all the noise. And between them, the teenagers and twentysomethings too cool for costumes. Other guys in trenchcoats or raincoats or sweatshirts slapped with huge logos. The girls in as little as they could manage while still keeping warm on a day that was slowly cooling and turning to drizzle. Everyone smiled brightly and yelled to the person next to them with strange enthusiasm and texted someone probably only across the street or a few blocks over. The entire world contained in this one maddening moment. And now the parade. Aging men and their made-up wives sliding by in their restored cars. Lines of policeman on horseback. Marching bands marching in time and blasting out songs that ricocheted between the brick buildings. That music and another band doing the same a few blocks up and a few blocks back and all of their steps and the crowd and the cars and the chanting march of uniformed children and every organization culminating in a mass of noise I could not escape.

29

FINALLY SAW THE VIDEO. **Rumors of it for** days. Of course no way to verify it. But everyone knew it was real. Low camera-angle, in the dark, a lantern nearby, a flashlight. You realize it's someone in a boat, and when the light comes it looks like the camera is pointing down a river. Because suddenly to the left, who knows how many miles away, a flash, the entire night lit up and all the light sucked away again and swallowed in a cloud at first of fire, and then dark. No sound. No sound of the victims crying out. They were already burned to death. No sound of the side who'd done this, rejoicing. They were far away, underground, they didn't need to be anywhere near. And then. Light on the other side of the river, further away, but the same kind of explosion, the same light and cloud taller than any mountains, and swallowed black again. And the same silence. Then, the camera man's gasps, his sobs, his tears, muttering a language I didn't know, made even more unknown through his tears. Boat on the water, wind, whispers, sobs. The world ended that way. Video ended with more lights, faster succession. Both sides. I doubt they've stopped yet, and won't until they're spent.

SOME OF THOSE MISSILES HAD TO HAVE BEEN OURS. Or at least our allies'. Which means whatever's been pointed at us for decades had to have finally been launched. Even assuming some of them were taken out before they could be launched. Or intercepted after they were launched. I'm talking out of my ass here, I don't know what anybody can do, I'm thinking of movies. But there are no reports yet of cities here being hit, on either coast. But I don't think they'd report it anyway. But it can't be long. We're not even in the top fifty for largest cities in the country, but three cities in the top ten aren't far away. Five and six hours east, and seven hours west. I don't know how far fallout would be but it can't be good to be in the middle. And the South ruined already with whatever disease. It'll jump over soon enough. If it hasn't already.

The border North is only four hours. If we had to, only a two hour or so drive and could cross on the lakes. This all assuming everyone else doesn't have the same idea. But would that be so bad? They aren't a nuclear power. But like anyone would even care, if this is the end. But it'd at least give us a moment. Keep going North. Colder. But alive.

COMPLETELY BIZARRE, THAT THOSE MISSILES WOULD BE USED. Why would they? Two years at least of ground war. Hardly any progress. But there's never any progress, on either side. Why would that be the option? Was it an accident? Is there actually a red button somewhere in those handful of countries, a little plastic guard you flip up to send the missiles flying? I feel like a child scribbling this. I don't know anything. I would think the world would feel different after this. But it doesn't. At least not here. Not yet. Birds, sidewalks, reruns, electricity. But the deaths of thousands or millions has never shifted the way people breathe, or made us walk either more bent or straight up, or made us speak more or less clearly or passionately. That's an insane thought, but an unavoidable one: that literally millions of people could be burned to death a continent over the water, and we're just going on.

MAINTENANCE GUYS WHEELING THEIR

HUGE PLASTIC DUMPSTERS ACROSS THE PARKING LOT, ALONG THE SIDEWALK. And that low gravelly rolling sounds like fireworks. And the fireworks we used to hear from the stadium nearby, always a sudden blast in a quiet night, made our suburb sound like a warzone. Fireworks echoing and reechoing and reverberating. High enough to light up our rim of trees but not high enough to see that they were fireworks, and they sounded like missiles or bombs or automatic weapons. Or at least what a warzone sounded like on TV, in night-vision green, what do I know. Pretty soon that's what it will be. And children not born will be curious we ever entertained ourselves with such sounds.

OLD WAR BOOKS SHOW AWFUL THINGS. Old women, black and white photos, in destroyed fields. Other old women and men all around. The field littered with corpses. Bent women looking for the bodies of their sons. Approaching women afraid to do so. Straightened women and men with their arms in the air, or crumpled men and women on the ground, having found what they feared.

And the thing is, I don't know how much of this can happen anymore. If they've been firing the worst missiles, why would any country not answer with the same? No ground war after that, no soldiers in any sense it used to mean. Just bombs dropped and answered, missiles fired. No search, because no recognizable remains, unless a piece of jewelry or some mark only a mother would know survives.

Assuming the mother didn't burn to death in the same fire that took her son.

These old pictures are bad enough. But worse is the same photo, same field, no one standing. Not even trees. Just charred lumps. Nothing to ever be found. Entire cities and families burned to death in a blast. The knowledge and history they held irretrievable. No way to recover the names. No way to mourn, except generally. Every individual detail shredded by flames.

THE AWFUL RADIANCE OF THE FIRST CARNAGE OF WAR IS SOMETHING I WILL NEVER KNOW. That the dead person will never know. That really no one knows for sure, that *This is the first dead body of a war.* Even that was more than two years ago. But there are no real starts to war, only continuations of old ones decades later.

But it's something I'll know some version of soon. A torn body. Lifeless and calm. On a road. Dozens or hundreds or thousands of them. That road is coming soon.

WHAT WILL HAPPEN TO THE REALLY OLD AND REALLY SICK I DON'T KNOW. With electricity and gasoline rare or gone, only the people who choose to stay will be bale to take care of those who can't move. And anyone with anything electrical, out of luck. So what then? Old age homes, coma patients, invalids, the sick? Not all of them will be burned to death in a flash. What? What?

A tray of poison shotglasses? A compassionate spray of automatic fire? With food entirely different and scarce, roads soon to be a mess, safety the first concern. What? Because I say, *People who choose to stay*, but where will the people who've left go? Where will I go? Just to another place somebody else has left?

Remember this old guy I knew, used to visit his wife in the home. She went far gone years before he did and he used to go see her a few times a week, though she never recognized him anymore. He'd always show up after dinner when her clothes were a little spattered. It'd be like she'd never seen him before and she would introduce her dolls to him, she was pretending they were her children.

And every time someone would say, *Your husband is here to see you!* And she would say she didn't have a husband. She was old and rambling and would say there was someone in the home she liked to watch movies with, *But I wouldn't even say he's my boyfriend, but yes we do talk.* Her husband's face would just fall at this, every time. But every time too he would have brought these laminated newspaper clippings. The two of them planted some sort of patriotic garden and the VFW had come out on Memorial Day, and they'd gotten in the paper for it.

Don't you remember that? he'd always ask her, and by this time she was annoyed and wouldn't look at him. She wanted to go back to her room. *How can you not—don't you remember our garden?*

I couldn't blame him for trying, I can't imagine that. He'd even touch her wedding ring and ask if she remembered when he gave that to her. But he'd always just end up outside in the parking lot, just standing there. I hope for his sake they're both dead by now.

STRANGE WAR DREAM. Was middle of the night, though I was going out to get the mail. Noticed my dad's car in the apartment garage, but I didn't see him anywhere. Got the mail and went by my own car. Driver's door open. This terrified me and I looked up and saw my apartment light come on. I drove away fast as I could. But then walking down a street towards an intersection from my hometown, now under construction. But you didn't see what it really was until you got right on top of the road, and a roadblock. Peering faces of tired construction workers, but then, across the way were lines of people being led over a bridge and thrown into a ravine that ran alongside the road and stopped just before the freeway. People going over and sprayed with automatic weapons. I noticed it was winter now. Roadwork machines and bodies in the snow. Steel and metal machines and bodies and body parts and faces peeking up through the light snow. I turned around and drove back to my apartment but there were more people in my place. An old-fashioned car with blonde teenage kids in the back getting out. Suddenly my mother is there and tells me we have to go. But suddenly we're inside with all of them and she's making everyone breakfast and asking me what I want. Giving me a look like we're just playing along until we can get out.

HOMELESS GUY ON THE BUS. **All the way in** the back. Whole bus reeked of piss. No telling when he'd gotten on or how long they'd let him stay. Rained all day so he was riding to keep dry. The drivers don't care anymore. But the guy was dressed something awful. No shirt that I could see. But a huge winter coat and what looked like sweatpants over jeans. No socks, but old tennis shoes. Some ratty collapsible cart covered in tarp blocking him into the back four seats. When I saw him he had a can of ravioli open and ate it cold with a plastic spoon, and slowly. What a prophecy.

DREAM. MOSTLY JUST IMAGES OF BEING IN DOWNTOWN, NOW JUST RUBBLE. Martial law of some government, or just thugs ruling it. I hid out in a library with some people while killing was going on outside. People scrambling all over inside the library. Some of them, I laughed in the dream to see it, to check their email, their phones. Got away from the people with guns with two or three other people and we hid in a rundown building. Looking out a broken window we saw an older man in a business suit, some kind of banker, looking terrified. Then we were crowded into a basement with a bunch of them, and the people with guns showed up and just starting slitting everyone's throat. One guy was so shocked by all of it that the slit appeared on his throat before it could be cut there.

BY THE BUS STATION. On the ground only a few feet from police officers in SWAT outfits and bullet-proof vests and lugging around automatic weapons was a homeless woman wrapped in a dirty white sheet. She was on her side and propped up by the bus stop she leaned against. As I approached her I couldn't make out just how her body was arranged beneath the sheet. All I could see was her head as it bobbed above and followed whatever passersby she could get a glimpse of. Frail bony hand that burst and seemed to float out from the sheet. A cup rattling with a few coins dangling from her fingers. The space that billowed out beneath her suggested her legs split off in all directions or that her body was inordinately larger than her head or that she had more than two arms, as if she were a spider. Had bulged eyes and a bloody nose. Hair matted down like an old dog's.

30

QUICK. BEFORE I FORGET. Things from the senses that I'll miss. Hearing: music from headphones. If this is as bad as it's supposed to be, birds of any kind. Animals. Cats. Annoying dogs barking at night. Baseball game broadcast on radio. Radio static when you drive under a bridge. Pummeling sound of freeway roadwork. Two-lane highways at night outside my window. Sound of wind in an office building. Ding of the elevator. Sound of phones. Huge crowds at a stadium. Skidding tires. Car. Bicycle. Skateboard wheels. People typing. Hair dryer. CD or DVD whirring before it starts playing. Come on. That can't be it. Sound of copier jamming continually for no fucking reason even after you've spent an hour going through it. Yeah. Sure. Miss that.

SEEING. HUGE VAST MOVEMENT OF PEOPLE AND THINGS DOWNTOWN. Buses and cars and pedestrians and taxis. Everyone rushing. Planes in the sky. People's changing wardrobe from season to season. Recognizing what people wear. People on corners waving. People in city streets with pieces of paper, lost. Casual people out for lunch. Walking with folded plate with piece of pizza sticking out. TV computer and movie screen. Phone screen. Smooth with no glare. Hills and streets around the house. Suburbs. I don't know. Half of this I won't know until I suddenly miss it. Photo albums I've already burned, I miss them already.

SMELL. SOME CRAPPY FAST FOOD HAMBURGER THAT'S SO HORRIBLE FOR YOU BUT SMELLS JUST INCREDIBLE, CHEESE AND BACON. New blacktop. Microwavable macaroni and cheese, twenty minutes, burned edges. Clean smell out of the shower. Soap and deodorant.

The middle of a sunflower. Cat litter. Superglue. Gasoline. Melting plastic. Smoking fajitas being brought to my table. Okay. No more food. Baseball mitt, worn leather. Inside of the car in summer. Honeysuckle. Smell of a good campfire. There will no doubt be more of those in the future but I'll miss the smell of them when they're rare and some kind of treat. Hand sanitizer. Smell of women's perfume.

TASTE. FOOD. Food. Food. I mean the crappy food we've all gotten used to eating. Sugar and salt. Cold pop. Cold beer. Apple juice. Those fajitas, side of rice and sour cream and refried beans. All of this will be possible I assume, just not in leisure. Just not a Wednesday after work before going home and lying around shirtless with my pants undone because I ate too much. A burrito. A pizza with steak onion and ranch. That same pizza with french fries instead of steak. Garlic bread. Meatballs. Steak. Going abroad and eating their food. Dessert. Peanut butter cup pie. Sticky toffee pudding with vanilla ice cream. I'm such a pig. So basic. Such a beast. Hot dog hamburger french fries. Bottle of four dollar wine. Six dollar vodka. Cup of ranch dressing for dipping. Syrup and pancakes, waffles. Breakfast! My God. Toast toasted just right with butter melted and strawberry jelly. Over easy eggs broken open over hash browns and sausage links. For real. Chinese food, noodles, broccoli, the sauces. Indian food, naan bread. Spices. Herbs. I'll miss the way I used to eat all of this. Or just the taste of my clean mouth, after brushing. Sweat on a woman's arm. Lips. Everywhere. The taste of having lost yourself and swallowed someone's body whole.

TOUCH. CLEAN CLOTHES. New clothes. Vacuumed couch. Soft cat, long hair. Barefoot in my apartment, linoleum and hardwood. Bathroom rugs under my feet after they've been washed. Old stuffed animals I threw away. A new book. Plastic unwrapping a new movie I just bought. All of our temporary packaging that just won't do. Styrofoam. Blue plastic cups. A good chair. A good recliner. A good bed. Good sheets. A woman's waist and how it curves to the hips. A woman's toes in my beard. Every silly touch. Tickles. And every amazing feat of physical contortion you never thought possible until you did it in the dark in the middle of the night. The touch of sweat after. Head on my shoulder. Legs and feet and arms all mixed up. Hair down her back or over her shoulder, my palm there. Hand cupping cheek and thumb to her lips. Kissed eyes. Great fortune and fearlessness. Sticking to the carseat in the summer. Feel of legs in the air propped up and body slouched in the movie theater. The feel of great laziness. Light switches and doorhandles and all the kinks in the windows and shades to get them open or closed. Of finally letting go what made her leave. What I couldn't convince myself of but so wanted to. So wanted to want it. The feel of the small vulnerable and warm weight of a child of ours, in my arms. The weight and heft of every-thing I must forget.

31

AND ALL I'LL MISS:

MOTHER CROSSING THE STREET EVEN THOUGH THE LIGHT IS GREEN. Pushing a stroller and on her cellphone. Two daughters she's not watching sort of following behind. One of them sees the green light. I see her glance up. Five years old and unsure about all of this and hurrying to her mother's side. And when she glances at her girl and then around for the other one she looks so sad and overwhelmed and annoyed. She looks so cherishing and indifferent, all at once. I'll miss these mothers and miss these children.

ALL THE DEBATES. I see young kids on the sidewalk clearly debating something. Should music be used in commercials? Fast food rock. Songs used to sell hamburgers and cars. Is that selling out? But some of the best music I've heard from the past few years, I first heard in cellphone commercials. I never thought I'd say it but I'll miss those debates, because those debates will go down. And so will the music. And so will the burgers and the cars and the phones. I'll even miss those kids on the street, debating as if the world depended upon their opinions of purity and right and sincerity.

BILLIE HOLIDAY SMOOTH AS ANYTHING AND THEN IN THE MIDDLE OF THE SAME WORD NINETY-DEGREES AND JUST WEIRD AND BROKEN AND CRUSHING. Break your heart. A good mass. A string quartet. Heavy metal my first record. Eastern European religious chanting where I hear my relatives' voices and the Russian Orthodox choir sounding nearly the same but distinct enough. The great bass voices, don't even need instruments, just a huge collection of voices. Break your heart. And then you float on it. And further east the same deep bass of Tibetan monks holding the syllables and holding the vowels like some Gregorian chant holding *Alleluia* for a minute. Latin or Russian or Tibetan, break your heart. Middle Eastern percussion or any percussion. Lines of drummers drumming a wedding or funeral song.

We know so well, we always have, how to make the moments of our lives, the stages and places, when to mourn and when to say, *We're awaiting on you all.* The dirge of strings or voice or organ or synthesizer. Suddenly uptempo brass or fast acoustic and footdrum and quick banjo. Full chorus of a hundred or just four faces around one microphone. Break your heart. Break your heart. And I can't read music. And at some point dead batteries and no power will swallow nearly all the music that's not in my head.

FAT MAN AT THE DOLLAR STORE. Button down shirt with top four, of course, unbuttoned. Bottom of sweaty neck and top of oily-hairy chest just a swamp, just what has already happened by noon on a weekday. And he's got missing teeth, a few. And he's wearing sweatpants. And he works there! Of course he does. He's working the cash register. And he knows everyone by name. This great bald meatball of a guy. How could I not miss him?

Nearing a bridge on the freeway. Heading downtown, rising. Look out the bus window. Some three-hundred feet away at the bottom of another clover-leaf of freeway. Another confluence of another handful of roads and freeways leading just as well somewhere else. From my seat three-hundred feet away and rising, angled up higher and sweeping away from them. The quick view of another bus. From overhead. A minivan. A sports car. More. All filled with souls going elsewhere who never saw me. A kind of view or realization impossible anywhere else or at any other point in history. I will miss those.

An old man who reminded me of the neighbor we had. In his nineties by now. A child of the shattered guys of 1918. A Marine later, must've been in the Pacific, old tattoo on his arm. Lived in his house sixty years, was there when they built it. Scratchy, irritable, always planting his vegetable garden every spring. Always challenging us to grow bigger tomatoes than him. Always talkative at all the wrong moments so I ignored or avoided him, and regretted it. Once told me he'd nearly been an

Olympic swimmer. Went to business college for just a second, tried to be a commercial pilot. But for sure sixty years with his vegetable garden and a string of Dalmatians he outlived and a million birdfeeders in every tree everywhere. Last I saw him he was hobbling and shuffling to his lawn-mower which he'd somehow turned over and set up on bricks. Some ancient box of tools at the ready. Still struggling. Still going. Always going. Gorgeous. I will miss him.

THOUGHT THAT I SAW MY WIFE'S STEP-MOTHER. My old mother-in-law. Same height and careful way of walking. Same short hair. Even the same kind of clothes. It's always struck me that we've all been here a million times already. But seeing this woman today, I'd say we're even here, right now, a thousand times. We're all in the faces and bodies and gestures and sounds of people we don't know. My mother-in-law never knew this twin. Probably as nice as her. Yet it's because of this stranger that I thought of her again.

I will miss everyone, so much. Strangers remind me of loved ones. And my loved ones remind others of their loved ones. Everything is everything. It isn't quite that easy or sentimental. But right now and especially in the future, it will be enough.

WE LOVE SO MUCH. There is so much to love. But it's so hard to do, to take that chance and give so much.

An old illustration I remember of a man opening his ribcage in some kind of pain, but also ecstasy. We can't get past the pain so we squander everything that's good. So that there's also so much to despise, to hate. But so much real loss to mourn, but so much that deserves punishment, that just sickens. Somewhere along the way the love is drowned and there's just what sickens. This makes no sense. All I mean is that we better realize again that love implies suffering. That there is no love without suffering. That there is value in suffering. If we don't find a way to see meaning in all the pain that's happened and the awful amount that's about to come we'll drown and deserve death.

A PARK JUST AS EVERYONE BEGAN SINGING A SONG. And kept singing it until everyone knew the words. Until everyone was in tears:

I am climbing high mountains trying to get home

I am climbing high mountains trying to get home

Lord I'm climbing high mountains

Well I'm climbing high mountains

Climbing high mountains trying to get home.

I am bearing the names of many trying to get home

I am bearing the names of many trying to get home

Lord I'm bearing the names of many

Well I'm bearing the names of many

Bearing the names of many trying to get home.

I am going down on my knees trying to get home

I am going down on my knees trying to get home

Lord I am going down on my knees

Well I'm going down on my knees

Going down on my knees trying to get home.

I am bearing hard burdens trying to get home

I am bearing hard burdens trying to get home

Lord I am bearing hard burdens

Well I'm bearing hard burdens

Bearing hard burdens trying to get home.

I am praying all I can trying to get home

I am praying all I can trying to get home

Lord I am praying all I can

Well I'm praying all I can

Praying all I can trying to get home.

I am taking all my crosses trying to get home

I am taking all my crosses trying to get home

Lord I'm taking all my crosses

Well I'm taking all my crosses

Taking all my crosses trying to get home.

32

My last night here. Hot water and electricity spotty. Spent the day washing some clothes and packing up. Took a long bath. Used up all the hot water I could, which wasn't much. Stayed in there for awhile, the window open. Hardly any sounds outside. At some point I broke down and sobbed. Covered my face in my hands. Lukewarm water and cold sweat burst open by the warmth in my cheeks and up to my eyes and it wouldn't stop. Pretended my wife was out for a hike, like she usually was. She'd come home any minute. I'd hold her from the tub. Hold her waist. Face to her thighs. But she never showed. I fell asleep and woke in the cold water later, and the lights were out.

A million memories of her but there's only how she couldn't lie when someone called on the phone for me and I would say as it was ringing, *If it's for me tell them I'm not here.* Every time she'd start to say it but just start laughing, *Oh he told me to say he's not here but he's right here.* I loved those laughing fits. So by the end I knew it was going to happen and would refuse to answer the phone and would just make faces and jump around when she answered and I was just dancing and being an idiot. She would just laugh harder.

I want whoever's left after to find

THESE UNSIGNED WORDS AND SAY THAT HERE WAS SOMEBODY WHO SAW IT HAPPENING. Someone with eyes open. Somebody who was not an asshole.

BEEN OUTSIDE FOR AWHILE. Think they said a school bus. Wonder how strict they'll be. Like an airport? Will they weigh my bag and see if it fits up top and tell me to get rid of some of it? Lights approaching slow. Must be them. Have to go.

OH MOTHER WHAT HAVE I LEFT OUT? Oh mother what have I forgotten?

.... **33**

AVOIDED FREEWAYS SO IT TOOK LONGER THAN IT MIGHT HAVE. Only drove during the day. It wasn't a school bus after all, but four or five minivans. School bus would draw too much attention. A full tank of gas got us the little more than two hundred miles to the border so we never had to stop for that. We figured a few things: people from South or West or East thinking the same as us would be driving hundreds more miles, wouldn't know where they were. So they'd take the freeways. Some might run out of gas, and clog the freeways. Those that didn't would scour the freeway gas stations clean in no time. So back-roads and non-chain gas stations and grocery stores for us. Found empty ones and took what we needed. Found ones still being run by living people, and played the game of giving them money.

NEARER THE LAKES AND THE BORDER THERE WERE FIRES ALL THROUGH THE NIGHT. City there we passed through when we reached it during the day mostly gone. Bodies in windows and on the street. Whoever had done this was long gone. We didn't think they'd gone over the border but continued further East. So even more reason to cross the border. One naked child dead in the road. Body twisted in some horrible angle, like a screw. If we'd come a few days earlier we'd have crossed with whoever did this. In the blackened windows and broken storefronts we all saw people peering up.

SAVAGE EARTH. Grassless ground. Treeless root. Sunless, blasted landscape. Suspended vine. Hanged men and women everywhere. Open, cracked field. Partial sprout. Narrow growth. Immediately exhausted energy spent in the sickened wind. Layered wind. The ash in it inseparable from it. The radiation. Like a lung lined with the soot of ages.

WHAT HAVE WE GIVEN? Each isolated in his own silent wood. An email. A home movie. An abandoned address. An old apartment. An untended grave. A ghost.

GOD IN THE COOL OF THE EVENING. Extinguishing each star as he passes. Turn off the lights now. The choir is done now. We've done all we can now. Just find a safe place please now. We'll wake you when we get there. When we start all over again.

34

THESE PEOPLE ARE ALL GOOD. They had no reason to take me on. Many of them with families, from the hospital. They knew I was alone and that I was not, so to say, terribly personable. But that's changing now. I can set to fixing things. If there's something practical with a mechanical solution I will find it. Like bottles of water or gasoline or batteries. I've been able to think up places to look for these things no one else has. Somebody asked the other night and I told them I'm not writing about myself here, so much as people. They liked that. They left me alone after that, and when I was done welcomed me back. I hesitate to say *into the fold*, but it might well be.

OVER THE BORDER A FEW DAYS NOW. Nobody at the check-points. Haven't seen anything all that uncommon. But the farther North we go it will get colder, and soon enough will be winter. That will be hard. A real test. Cans and bottles and jars, cans and bottles and jars. As much as we can find. A few of the people hunt. There's no more local meat than this. I offered to learn. Found a lot of local maps. If we can find a secluded place for the winter that will be enough. On a height, or defensible spot somehow, if it needs to be. No one wants to talk too much about that. It's true that if it's isolated enough few people are liable to care, to want to come and kill everyone and take our things. The old thought that the worst violence might actually happen in removed places doesn't have as much support as before. Rumor is that the ten most populous cities I mentioned a long time ago are all gone, and who knows what else. Nobody I don't think will care much about twenty-five or thirty people and their cans of peaches.

SOME OF THE CELL TOWERS STILL WORKING. Not sure how or why. So when we find one everyone racks up their data they'll never pay for to see if there's any news. Very little certain. News feeds from the middle of nowhere, back home or in Europe. Hundreds of miles away from bombed cities, telling us news of those bombed cities. But who knows where they heard about it. Every now and then a picture of a corpse in a bathtub or what looks like an entire neighborhood crouched in a dried out riverbed. Ran there after the fire fell, their bodies falling apart and looking for cool water. Just charred people. But could just as well be people dead from disease. I always heard those cases were desperate for cold water to jump in and dunk. Maybe they'd had the double indignity of getting sick and then being bombed. Or getting sick and then just slaughtered by somebody, and then set to with a flame-thrower. All guesses.

AROUND THE FIRES AT NIGHT EVERYONE JUST TALKS. At some point stories. There's nothing and no one else but each other to look at or listen to.

Someone remembers the pizza place he used to order from all the time. Walkup from his house. Been going there since he was a kid. The same people always there, middle-aged women who got older, cooks and owners. How they talked in quick little gossip or some inside joke or sneered at the difficult customers, and did so right in front of them too. Mock-quarrels between themselves. Said it was amazing to watch them shuffle and sit and bustle in old routine, for years.

Another remembered being a waitress, and jealous of some rich emphysema-ridden old man. Always coughing up a lung. Always had a brand-new yellow car outside. How he got in an car accident once and just bought a new one like it was nothing, lucky bastard. Showed up a week later with the new car like it was the old car. But how now he's probably just sick and alone, if he's still alive at all.

In her absence I deserve these people, I think. I've always wished for something like these evenings, I've always wanted it, but have only gotten it in a charnel ground.

35

PEOPLE ARE GETTING UGLIER. So much uglier.
If a woman has a shape anymore you wouldn't know from
the piles of clothes we all wear now. But you can tell by
the hands and the faces that it's not a concern. No movie-
star men either. No smooth-shaven-ocean-smelling cheeks
from the commercials. No woman with her perfect finger-
nails and hands and perfect white teeth throwing her arms
around his shoulders and gasping at the smooth cheeks and
the dumbfuck architecture of chiseled facial hair.

Two years ago we were still worried about a nation of fat
kids. Now no jewelry, no style, no way yet with clothes or
anything else to distinguish by class or power or anything.
Someday that will happen again. Someday archaeologists
will suddenly note the return of richer burials and people
with more grave goods than others and some graves on a
height or in a mound or including some special structure
and all the rest. They'll note that in this strata here, you
can see it, the whole dumb show started all over again. We
just can't help it.

EVERY DEATH IS A LOSS NOW. I'm ashamed to
have ever thought otherwise. All bitterness is gone.

THINGS JUST DON'T HAPPEN TO MOST PEOPLE.
I'm sure somewhere else there's a congress of hardasses

gathered, and their group contains some example of every race or whatever, symbolic of all society, deciding what to do when somebody comes to take whatever they have. Whatever the big decisions are.

But not here. Most people will just live or just die. The quiet energy of simple intimacy. That kind of anonymous power will outlive us more than our names. There's someone in Pakistan writing this. In Russia. In France. Dubai. South Africa. Belize. Across the way. There's always been somebody writing this.

36

CONVERSATION WITH A WONDERFUL WOMAN TONIGHT. Glasses. Took her hat off when I took off mine. Strange new formalities that are actually really old, coming back. Brown hair grown just past her shoulders, though she said by now she usually would've gotten it cut. She saw I had glasses and that's what made her say hello.

What happens if our glasses break?

I know. Feel bad for the people with contacts.

I'm blind without these.

Me too.

Here, let me see. And she reached her hand out and touched my face as she took my glasses off. Fingertips just barely touching beside my eyes.

She didn't take hers off and waited for me to do it. So I could touch her face. Astounding contact. Everything was a blur but I could see her smile. I can't imagine what kind of smile I wore. I took her glasses like I was going to put them on and I said, I don't want to break them on my huge head, stretch them out.

Oh stop.

She said she'd been walking with the group since we'd left the city. How I didn't see her before I don't know. We've gathered a few more people but I usually see everybody new but I didn't see her.

Played the game of having our glasses off and moving our faces closer and closer until they finally became clear. To see how horrid our eyes really are. Nothing in all of my longing could compare to the second her face came into focus in front of mine. The great smile from my years of hunger.

SAW HER AGAIN TODAY. Last night she went back to where she was sleeping like we were fifteen and her parents said we couldn't sleep in the same room yet. I saw her throughout the day but knew she'd come back after dark when the only light were fires. Said she saw me writing in this book and asked if I had written about her. I said of course I had. She asked what else there was and I started reading to her at random, all that I've told you here.

I went back and forth. Or flipping the pages and she put a finger down as the pages flew by. By the end of the night we'd both cried, and her hand was in mine. The world I'd written about only pages before was already so far away.

How in this half-dead world she came to me because I was wearing glasses, I have no idea. How in this half-dead world where everyone is more desperate and in need and are more kind. The awful daring of a moment's surrender that would've been impossible otherwise. The worst starvation, disease, violence, are all on the fringes. Like frayed ends of fabric that will catch fire any moment. They will all be here in a moment. And the elements. There's no avoiding any of them, variations of them, even worse. But amid and between she suddenly appears. No more perfect than me. No savior. No goddess. But simply the most beautiful gestures and intentions, heart. Her hand is everything. Sleeping breath. The warmth of another soul stretching beside me.

Would you have approached me?

You mean before this started?

Yeah.

I don't know. I would've written about you. I would've seen you.

What if you had approached me?

What do you mean?

Where would we have gone?

Ideal situation? No limits?

The sky.

Okay. England.

You would've seen me at the diner and asked me out, and then taken me to England?

I would've loved to have done that.

And where would we go? Away from the big cities?

If you wanted.

And then?

Small towns in the north. We'd take a train there.

And then just walk around? Shop?

We'd look but not buy much. It would be enough to be there, to know smaller places. Talk to the people. We'd have spent all our money on the flights and the train.

No going back?

Why come back here?

But no hotel even?

Who knows, camping somewhere.

Let's say we at least had enough money to go out to eat.

Okay.

You like Italian?

Who doesn't?

So we'd find a good Italian place. And we'd get there before anyone else. Have the place to ourselves.

That's right. It would be perfect for us, an empty place. And dessert. A few beers.

But then something surprising would happen.

What's that?

A band would start setting up. We'd have been there for two hours already, and the place is filling up.

What? Rock band? Some guy and his acoustic?

Jazz.

Quartet?

Yes.

What then?

We'd watch them set up, and wonder if we should stay. A small stage, they'd be moving the piano around and setting up their drumkit and we would just laugh when we saw the standup bass, how tall they are. And we would stay.

We would. The crowd wouldn't bother us anymore. We'd be right up front. A huge crowd of people behind us and we wouldn't feel nervous at all. And until then we'd have been sitting on opposite sides of a table.

That's no fun.

But you'd be on the booth side. And at some point I'd come over and join you.

That would be fabulous.

And I'd put my arm around you.

If I didn't put my arm around you first.

You'd smile at me.

I would.

And we'd notice an older couple in the room.

We would? What about them?

Old English couple. People who fell in love during the Blitz, and listening to that music was like reliving their courtship. That's what they would mean to us. Old love still there. Unbroken.

Ghosts?

I wouldn't mind ghosts like that.

Even death doesn't part them. They show up in town and go to their favorite joint for music.

We'd be okay with ghosts.

We would.

And we'd take a taxi back.

A taxi? Where? To our tent?

Somewhere beside a lake. Mountains. Stone walls crawling all over the mountains. That would be our first date.

She put her arm around me and smiled and kissed my scraggly beard. Thank you for the evening. I had a wonderful time.

Ages since I wrote here. So much has happened. The worst and the best. But this had to be set down. Came across a main street somewhere that hadn't been looted all the way yet. Somehow two of our guys found some musical instruments. A fiddle and a guitar. Played for us all night. One song was perfect, I don't know what it was. Started just the guitar but then the fiddle came in. But it was all there. Longing. Fulfillment. Meaning. Emotion. Disappointment. Growth. Perseverance. Reflection. All of it bittersweet. All a dialogue of guitar and fiddle. Not complete contentment. Not endless suffering. No sense of giving up. All a beautiful mixture.

And the end has the fiddle trail off to leave the last note from the guitar. And on that last note and just before our applause the fiddler smiled and said, *Yesss!* And what he said with that syllable was, *Yes, you've captured this mixture of sadness and joy. How awfully hard life is. How high the highest joy and how low the worst sadness. How there is nothing but the mixture of these. You've captured it, and for that we are happy.* And we are. This is all we have.